Frannie o

FRANNIE
on the
Orient Express

by

Francesca Jones

WARNER BOOKS

A *Warner* Book

First published in Great Britain
by Warner in 1994

A CIP catalogue for this book
is available from the British Library

ISBN 0 7515 1015 7

Photoset in North Wales by
Derek Doyle & Associates, Mold, Clwyd
Printed and bound in Great Britain by
Clays Ltd, St Ives plc

Warner
A Division of
Little, Brown and Company (UK) Limited
Brettenham House
Lancaster Place
London WC2 7EN

For my son, James –
with all the love in the world.

1

THE HUNT BALL

LORD BALLINGTON'S FACE WAS AVERTED from the spray of small clumps of damp mud and grass which the thundering hooves of the chestnut mare in front of him were throwing up, but that did not prevent his eyes from persistently straying to the delightful derrière of its rider; Frannie, Lady Ballington, lovely face glowing from the excitement of the chase, was standing on her stirrups and leaning over the horse's powerful neck, the thin, palest-of-beige material of her riding breeches stretched enticingly tight over her perfectly moulded, infinitely desirable buttocks.

Galloping with boisterous enthusiasm a few yards to Victor Ballington's right was the handsome, debonair and notorious American playboy Neville Duke, a first-time house guest at Stratton Castle over the extensive grounds of which – an estate comprising one eighth of the county of Wiltshire and owned by Lord Ballington – the hunt was taking place. As Victor's worldly-wise, slightly cynical grey eyes slid from his wife's backside to rest momentarily on the American he perceived that his guest's gaze was rooted on the same anatomical feature which his own had just left; he smiled to himself as a risqué idea began to take shape in his remarkably sexually fertile brain.

Up ahead, the excited pack of hounds scrambled under, over and through an ancient wooden fence. Seconds later, their riders' colourful coat tails flying, the horses were taking the unformidable obstacle in their stride.

Shortly after, the hounds lost the scent and the hunters reined in their sweaty mounts; horses and riders milled around in the crisp, April morning air as the pack of dogs, noses to the ground, tails waving, barking and yelping, ran around on the banks of a shallow ditch either up or down which the fox had evidently run.

Puffing from his exertion – though at fifty-four he was exceptionally fit and appeared some ten years younger – the craggily aesthetic-looking Lord Ballington drew his steed up by the side of Neville Duke's. Both stallions were panting heavily, their flanks curtained with foamy, white perspiration; their nostrils flared, their ears were pricked up and they were impossible to hold still, filled, as they were, with the excitement of the gallop.

'Wonderful morning, Victor. Fantastic country-side. And you've supplied me with one hell of a fine horse,' said Neville as his stallion whinnied and performed a tricky little dance beneath him.

'I try to surround myself with pleasing things, but I can't take credit for the weather.' The Ballington eye shrewdly appraised his American guest. At thirty – just two years older than Frannie – Neville Duke was a young man to make female hearts flutter. Tall in the saddle, broad shouldered, he cut a fine figure in his tailored riding outfit. He had a strong-featured, swarthy face and piercingly dark eyes whose curling lashes were almost as long as those of his horse. Tight black, shiny curls were bunched below his hard hat to half cover his ears and lap over the back of the velvet collar of his hunting jacket. His gaze wandered over the restless, colourful scene to fall on Lady Ballington who was laughing with the only other woman present, a well-known, sturdy looking baroness.

'You are possessed of extraordinarily good taste. I congratulate you,' Neville commented.

'Why, thank you. I suppose, at this moment, you are referring to my choice of wife?'

The American's eyes, lazily smiling, swivelled back to those of his host. 'I have to hand it to you. She's lovely.'

'Horse flesh, woman flesh – they should both be selected with the greatest of care.' He paused. 'I utterly adore Frannie, Neville.'

'I didn't mean to suggest. . .'

'But it's perfectly all right, Victor interrupted mildly. 'There'd be something seriously wrong with you if you didn't fancy her.'

'But, my dear friend . . . ' The American's habitual silky-smooth urbanity found itself jolted.

'And knowing her as I do I'd wager my entire stable against a pig's snout she's got the hots for you.'

Neville's long lashes blinked rapidly. He stared blankly at Lord Ballington, mouth dropping open. 'You don't say?' he muttered, confused, and then he had a little fight to restrain his horse, which was raring to take up the chase.

'She's studying you now. I know that look very well. Admiring you. Speculating.'

Which was perfectly true. She grinned at Victor, pretty green eyes dancing momentarily on him before floating back to Neville as he got his horse under control. Her grin faded and she raised an eyebrow as she glanced once again at her husband and ran her tongue over her lips. Pure understanding passed between them.

Neville Duke was too much the experienced man of the world to be thrown off balance for long by Victor's insinuations; it would not be the first time – and it seemed to him that that was exactly what was happening at this moment – that an older man had offered him his young and beautiful wife for sexual purposes. 'Speculating about what?' he asked.

'The same thing as you yourself were as you looked so longingly at her buttocks during the last gallop.'

'I see. And. . .?'

'And we now find ourselves on the same wavelength, do we not?'

The horn put an end to the conversation; the hounds had picked up the scent of their quarry and were off. The hunters spurred their eager mounts into a brisk canter behind them. For a mile they charged over open grassland, before jumping a hedge, then a ditch, and threading their fast, perilous way through a copse. The riders came upon the pack with the fox cornered in a hollow beneath a tree, spread out around the

4

hounds and stopped.

Frannie disengaged herself from her companions. She was panting, face radiant, adrenalin seething – but she walked her mare away from where the bloody death was about to take place. As his stallion bumped Neville's in the crush around the oak tree, Victor said, 'Frannie detests the actual kill. But she'll be tense with excitement at this moment.' He glanced across at Lady Ballington, eyes narrowing, then back at the American. 'Why don't we two take advantage of that fact?'

'Advantage?' Neville glanced at his chunky gold watch. It was five to eleven. He raised a thick eyebrow. 'Whatever you say.' Assuming that this unusual species of British aristocracy could mean only one thing by that remark, but curious that he was suggesting a sexual romp at that hour of the day, he ambled his now weary horse behind Victor's and they joined Frannie.

'Keyed up, darling?' Lord Ballington asked his wife.

'I'll say,' she told him. 'But you know how I hate the kill.'

'I don't go much for it myself,' said Neville.

'But you go for Frannie?' Victor wiped sweat from his forehead with the back of a gloved hand and in so doing smeared a dab of mud across it.

Duke kept his cool. 'So you keep telling me.' His eyes caught Frannie's, holding them. 'So he keeps telling me.'

'*Really*, Victor,' Frannie playfully admonished, nostrils slightly flaring, not breaking her eye contact with the American. 'This is supposed to be a hunt.'

'We caught the fox. Now we're after you.'

'Is your husband always – ah – like this?' asked Neville, grinning boyishly, beginning to get into the spirit of the sexual game. His nose twitched as he caught a whiff of Frannie's fragrant perfume.

'He has a tendency to be flippant,' she said, jutting out her chin. 'I do wish you'd learn to behave yourself, Victor.'

'I doubt that. And I'm not being flippant. I'm being most serious. Neville was taking more interest in your delectable haunches than those of any horse or, indeed, in the hunt itself. I repeat – *we* are after you.'

'I can't imagine what you mean.'

'Then we shall have to show you.'

The dogs' barking swelled to a cacophonous din; the pack leader had almost scraped away enough earth from between the roots of the ancient oak for them to get at their quarry. Lord Ballington glanced briefly in the direction of the imminent kill; then, his mind definitely on something else he treated his wife to a most lubricious look, stripping her with his eyes. He urged his horse forward, away from the hunt and the other two followed. He silently led the way until they were crossing a clearing where he said, walking his stallion on one side of Frannie, Neville on the other, 'As I recollect, there's a ruined mill house in this direction.'

'Is there now? And just what do you propose we do there?' Frannie's pulse was thumping. It may have been only eleven o'clock on a bracing morning but the suggestive conversation had served to stir her sexual juices; besides, she found the American extremely attractive.

'You,' said Victor. 'We are going to do you.'

'Me,' muttered Frannie, weakly.

'Will you now confess to having been excited by the sight of my wife's enticing bottom, Neville?'

'Okay. Who wouldn't be?'

'You are a red-blooded swordsman, as I understand it?'

'Swordsman?'

'A womaniser.'

He grinned. 'I guess.'

'Red-blooded enough to get it up on a chilly April morning?'

Taking a deep breath, his eyes wandering over Frannie who, mind in somewhat of a turmoil, was now keeping hers fixed straight ahead, Neville responded to the challenge. 'You bet,' he said lustily.

They reached the far side of the clearing and were once again obliged to walk the horses in single file through the trees. Victor twisted in the saddle to look at Frannie who was in front of Neville. 'I see that our guest's eyes are invading your bum again, my lady. Then we shall bare it for him in the mill – would you not agree?'

Frannie swallowed hard. Fire was kindling deep in the pit of her belly. 'It'll get cold,' she said, very quietly.

Her husband thwacked his riding crop against his boot; the sharp crack startled a small flock of sparrows which rose from the trees in a screeching crowd. 'Then we shall warm it up for you. A few swipes of this followed by a lively rogering should see to that.'

'God.'

The word 'rogering' was not in the American's vocabulary – but he got the idea all right. He could not see the curves of Frannie's backside at that moment because her flared jacket had them covered. His imagination, though, had shifted into top gear; already his penis was stirring in anticipation of the frolic to come.

The three riders emerged from the copse in silence, each one's mind filled with thoughts of imminent sex. At the bottom of a gentle slope before them, straddling a fast-running stream, the ruined mill house stood in weak sunshine.

On the edge of the stream next to the ruin there was a solitary willow tree. Dismounting, saying very little, the preoccupied trio allowed their horses to have their fill to drink, then tethered them to the branches of the tree. As Frannie loosened her mare's girth she became aware of Victor's hand sliding down the back of her jacket. He reached beneath it for her bottom. As his fingers searched deep beneath her crotch and squeezed he muttered, lips close to her ear, breath scorching it, 'Are you ready for this?'

Looking over her shoulder she found within his eyes the cocktail of amusement and lust with which she was so familiar. She turned around, his rummaging hand going with her. Lifting her knee so that her thigh pressed into his crotch to crush his as yet flaccid penis into his testicles, excitement as tense as that of the hunt surging through her, she said, 'You're the boss. Me – I'm ready for anything.'

Neville Duke's eyes narrowed on the two of them as he finished sliding his stirrups up their leathers so that they would not irritate the horse by hanging loose against its flanks. Victor's free hand, he noticed with great interest, had found its way inside Frannie's jacket to maul her breasts. 'I guess maybe I'd better just leave you two to it?' said Neville.

'Absolutely not. You're our guest, remember? The reason for the coming party.' Releasing Frannie's sexual parts and backing his own off her thigh he took the hand of his now extremely aroused wife and led her along the river bank towards a large, jagged and crumbling hole in the mill brickwork where once there had been a door. 'And Frannie is the hostess,' he threw over his shoulder as the American followed them.

It was shadowy inside the building. The noise of the stream which surged beneath it was echoey, magnified by the old walls. Victor took them to the centre of the ruin, to where a huge millwheel, its lower paddles which would otherwise be immersed in the water broken away, was rusted into position on its race. The wheel's heavy axle rested in worn grooves in stone walls on either side of the stream, but the millstones had long since disappeared to grace the walls of a pub in the nearby village. Victor turned his wife's back to the wall and eased her against it; its uneven top edge indented her buttocks.

Lord Ballington removed his hard hat and put it on the wall. The American had left his with his horse; his thick crop of shiny black curls hung unrulily around his face in contrast to Victor's disciplined grey hair. Tensely waiting, eyes flickering expectantly from one man to the other, hands flat beside her on the wall, belly fluttering, Frannie was hornily aware that she was alone with, and about to be sexually indulged by, the two most handsome men of the hunt; the fact that one was her husband and twenty-six years older than her merely added to the thrill.

Making a show of yanking his riding crop from his boot, Victor Ballington ran its springy, tasseled end up the inside of Frannie's thigh until it reached her crotch, poked it between her legs and put pressure on it, bending it upwards. She was keenly aware of its steel-cored strength against her pussy as, jiggling it there, he grated, 'You and I have at our disposal, Neville, the most perfect example of British womanhood. We shall have our wanton way with her.' He bent the end of the crop even harder under her pubis, then he began to slide it upwards. 'Getting wet, your ladyship?' he hissed, eyes smouldering.

Her pouty lips slackened, her eyes drooped. 'Yes,' she whispered.

Victor's eyes slid to those of the American who was watching this sex play with cock almost gone solid and beginning to strain against his breeches. 'Wet, hot, and very horny,' he told him. 'She has no restraint, my dirty wife, which fact is deserving of punishment. But first, let's free her tits.' He ran the tip of the crop up to her cheek. 'What say you, Francesca?'

Frannie could only whimper as Victor deftly unfastened her waistcoat buttons. He insinuated the tip of the crop through her crisp, white shirt and prodded her navel with it as, sliding right into a playfully sado-sexual mood he hooked his fingers under her shirt collar – between it and her neatly tied black stock with its ruby-headed holding pin – and ripped the shirt open so roughly from neck to waist that he tore off three of its pearl buttons in the process.

Neville Duke grunted in raunchy appreciation as Frannie's glorious tits, pinkish nipples pointed and hard, fell free, trembling. Victor moved the crop tip up from her naval to flick its leather tassels over each nipple as he muttered, 'The most perfect boobs in the county, Neville.' He stood back. 'Why don't you help yourself to a handful?'

The American moved in on her, eyes agleam as if there were hot embers in their black depths. He stripped off his calf gloves, stuffed them in his pocket and grabbed, flattening a palm over each quivering tit, tightening his fingers over them as his loins crushed into Frannie's belly and his lips ground against hers. Almost of its own accord, her eager hand ferreted down between their bodies to discover his impressively hard cock as their tongues wetly mingled. Standing to one side, closely observing this last action, Lord Ballington said loudly, 'She has not the *slight*est restraint. My dear wife should have been a whore.'

Breaking the embrace, moving back a pace but keeping his hold on Frannie's breasts and rolling them together, her crumpled nipple area poking through the spaces between index fingers and thumbs, Neville drooled, 'My God, is she the hottest of stuff!'

'You are so right, my friend. But before she *gets*

stuffed we'll warm her up even more. Take down her breeches, why don't you?'

As Frannie's knees weakened and her insides turned to jelly, the American took his prurient time about unstudding the sides of her skin-tight riding trousers and easing them down to her knees; the tops turned themselves over to flop over her hand-made, muddy boots. She was wearing high cut, white, silky panties from her favourite lingerie supplier – New York's Bonni Keller. They had a broad band of fancy lace around their legs and there was the suspicion of the shadow of her bush beneath them. Neville, experienced man of the world that he was, assuming that a part of Lord Ballington's pleasure in the sharing of his wife was dictation of the proceedings, looked up at him and raised a thick, questioning eyebrow.

'But of course,' murmured Victor. Seconds later Frannie's knickers had joined her trousers at her knees. She leant her head back and half closed her eyes. Her hand slipped over her taut little belly until the tips of its emerald-lacquered nails were straying amongst the uppermost, light brown curls of her downy pubic thatch. In great sexual need as she was, the hand nevertheless stilled; Lady Ballington was almost – but not *quite* – ready to play with herself in front of this almost stranger. With her other hand she groped for the stud in the strap of her helmet; the strap was digging slightly into her neck. Victor stopped her from undoing it. 'I want to have you in disarranged, but full riding gear,' he insisted. 'Including the hat. In other words, the perfect, aristocratic slut.'

Alone, with this beautiful vision of bawdiness,

the American would have known exactly what was required of him. His eyes were fixed gloatingly on her pussy but he no longer touched her. He was uncomfortably aware of a healthy throbbing in his cock, which begged for freedom. 'I, ah, I guess I need to . . . ' he muttered, hand going to his zip fly.

'And I,' said Victor. 'But she may not watch. She's turned on quite enough as it is.' Taking Frannie by her upper arm he spun her around. Then he put a hand on the back of her neck and coaxed her down over the wall. 'Bend,' he ordered. 'Spread your legs as much as you are able and let us see your backside in the same position as when you were galloping – but this time in all its rude, naked glory.'

Frannie stretched her arm along the millwheel axle and gripped the rusty metal for support as she was doubled over the ancient wall. Her gaze became fixed on the turbulent stream below her. Her heart pounded. Her pussy was agreeably wet – and the knowledge of what a salacious view of her parts she was presenting to the two men was making it wetter by the second.

'Now,' said Victor Ballington, loud enough so that his wife could hear him over the noise of the stream which now filled her ears, ' . . . I suggest we get out of our boots and breeches and treat that bottom to the sound thrashing it so richly deserves before poking my lady – and her arse, if you happen to be so inclined.'

While Frannie, wound up like a tight clock-spring, vaguely watched the sparkling water as it rushed through the mill, the men helped each other off with their boots then climbed out of their breeches and underpants and put them on the wall. The sexual heat in them served to keep their naked loins warm but it was too cold to remove their red hunting jackets. Big hard-ons sticking through their shirt tails and wobbling, they approached Frannie's bare, tasty rump with riding crops in hand.

Her buttocks were tensed against the first blow but Frannie had no idea when it would fall since she could not see the men; Victor delivered it, measuring his aim carefully before cutting the crop sharply through the air. It bit neatly across both cheeks of her bottom, the shock of the sharp pain bringing a shriek to Frannie's lips. Her feet jumped from the ground so that all of her weight was for the moment on her belly on the stone and she jerked her head so violently that her hard hat broke free to fall into the stream and be carried away. Her hair, loosely pinned high, began to shake down. The second slash, delivered by the enthusiastic Neville Duke to paint a thin red stripe diagonally across that made by her husband, convulsed her again and her thick and wavy blonde hair tumbled down about her ears.

It was pain, yet it was a sweetly arousing hurt and welcomed since it had been some while since her last whipping. As her buttocks began to glow and the glow spread within her to further inflame her libido Frannie's shrieks changed to gasps of pure pleasure. Her free hand stole between her legs and her castigators were offered the additional, ribald enjoyment of the sight of two of her fingers working energetically in her pussy

14

while Frannie brought herself to swift, ecstatic orgasm as the riding crops lashed her behind; her legs suddenly stiffened, her entire body went as rigid as the mens' cocks, she shouted, the knuckles of the hand gripping the rusty bar went white, and the fingers in her pussy stilled.

Lord Ballington stopped the American's hand as he lifted it to deliver another blow. 'Enough,' he muttered. 'She is now wonderfully ripe for a fucking – and I don't want her cut.' He ran the tassels of his crop down the crack in Frannie's behind to jiggle them on her pussy where her fingers remained half-buried. 'After you, dear boy,' he invited.

Neville dropped his crop, took a hold of his cock and closed in on Frannie's smarting, blushing, multi-striped bottom as Victor carefully laid his riding crop across the wall. Bending slightly at the knees behind Frannie the American unhanded himself to spread her vulva with both thumbs. Positioning the swollen head of his cock without touching it he heaved into her, its topside cramming against fingers slippery with her juices.

As his prick began to pound, his pelvis bumping into her tortured buttocks, Frannie became quickly aroused from her post-climax lethargy. Her fingers slipped from their cock and pussy sheath and their tips found her clitoris. She raised her head. Orgiastic arousal once more beginning to grip her, she became vaguely aware that she was looking at – three fields away, through a jagged hole in the ruin – the main body of the hunt, hounds scampering around them as they made their way home.

What was so steamily taking place in the old mill was exactly the sort of sexual scene in which the Ballingtons revelled; watching Frannie get screwed by a handsome young man was one of Victor's greatest pleasures, as, indeed, having it done to her while he looked on was one of hers. Consumed with lust – and with a mounting craving to join in the action – his lordship glanced around the ruin, searching. His eyes alit on a group of wooden barrels which had, decades since, been used to transport ground corn. His fertile, libidinous mind went to work. Crossing to the corner where the heavy barrels were stored he tipped one of them on to its side and rolled it until its end was touching the wall close to the rutting pair. Caring little now about the cold he took off his jacket and rolled it up; he laid it on the worn, red brick floor on one side of the barrel and spread both of the riding breeches on top of one another.

'Neville,' he said. Then again, louder, because his voice had been drowned by the American's impassioned grunts, Frannie's panting, and the rushing sound of the stream, 'Neville?'

The heavy, hairy buttocks stilled. In any case approaching the point of no return and a man who by nature liked to drag out his sexual enjoyment for maximum pleasure, he had been about to make the considerable effort of holding back his orgasm. Neville turned his head to follow Victor's suggestive tilt of his chin; he immediately understood. Taking a firm grip of Frannie's dangling breasts he pulled her upright. Dipping further at the knees, his cock fully impaled in her and balls hanging under her pussy, he walked her to the barrel where his hands left her breasts to climb to her shoulders and push. As she sank down he went with her until they were both kneeling on the breeches, genitally locked, and her belly and tits were squashed into the smooth, blackened wood and a broad, cold, rusted iron hoop of the barrel.

Lord Ballington, fist wrapped around his needful hard-on – on which his wife's lust filled eyes were greedily locked – dropped to his knees on his hunting jacket. Grabbing hold of his backside, Frannie opened her scarlet lips wide and, tongue slightly protruding over the nether one, she took as much of Victor's cock between them as her mouth could accommodate.

Frannie – literally – over a barrel, on this crisp, early spring morning! The swallows who nested in what remained of the eaves of the ruined mill played host to activity as lubricious as that depicted in any pornographic magazine. The beautiful, glamorous Lady Ballington, toast of Wiltshire, London-tailored riding breeches and Christian Dior knickers – their label inside out – at her pretty, dimpled knees, hunting jacket, waistcoat and shirt in an untidy pile high up near her shoulders, is raunchily fucked doggy style by a well-known American playboy who is naked from the waist down but still sporting his red jacket, whilst she avidly sucks on her husband's heavy, rampant dick. With each hefty thrust of Neville Duke's buttocks, as his swollen balls crush between the soft tops of Frannie's milky thighs, the barrel rolls slightly forward; as he withdraws and briefly pauses, smouldering gaze ogling the glans-impaled object of his penetration, it rocks back, faintly creaking.

The strong American hands are spread over the luscious, bare, British bottom, its thumbs between superbly rounded cheeks. Remembering Victor's hint that this bum may be buggered if he is so inclined – and he happens to be most partial to that particular sexual variation – Neville digs his thumbs in close to Frannie's anus and with them stretches it open. He finds it uncommonly tempting, her puckered and pale brown little hole. Uncoupling from her pussy, cock good and slippery with vaginal juices, he attempts to enter it. But his glans is large and thick and Frannie's bottom hole tiny and delicate. A heave which contrives half the cockhead in makes her grunt in pain on her mouthful of cock. The toes of her boots drum on the stone floor. She jerks her head back, her lips slide off Victor's prick and she gasps, as Neville stretches her sphincter even more, 'No. Stop – *stop*. Not without oil or something.' Then as Neville ceases his effort her relief is tinged with disappointment as Victor grunts, 'Leave it. We have no lubricant.'

Neville regretfully goes back to poling Frannie's pussy. The threesome heats up. A communal orgasm begins to overtake it. The barrel rocks faster, its creaking growing louder, sounding almost like bedsprings. Frannie frantically gobbles cock as Neville's grasping hands slide from her buttocks to her waist and one of them bumps over the knobs of her perfectly white spine to bury itself in the hair at the nape of her neck as his belly meets her back and he rams home his climactic thrusts. Victor is leaning back, hands resting on Frannie's head with its tumbling, disarrayed hair, showing his teeth in a sexual grimace, eyes closed; she needs to do no more than sway with the roll of the barrel for her lips to slide up and down his cock.

Climax seethes through them; it begins with Neville's sperm erupting from his balls into Frannie's cunt which reacts by clamping his prick in a fierce contraction; it grips Frannie in the pit of her belly, then rushes through her body from one end to the other, causing her toes to curl in her boots and her mouth to suck on Victor's cock with the force of a vacuum pump; it reaches a lengthy, shuddering, utterly consuming end with Lord Ballington's sperm pouring into Lady Ballington's mouth to trickle from its corner, run down her chin and drip on to his jacket; it retreats.

Frannie unmouths her husband, gulps down his semen, raises her head and, tensely trembling in the final throes of what has been a string of orgasms, howls at a swallows' nest; a startled bird pops out of the nest to swoop towards the source of its disturbance before veering away and gliding through a hole in the ruin.

The hunt ball is over.

2

CHEEKY EYES

HAD MY INIQUITOUS ENCOUNTER WITH Neville Duke not taken place it is doubtful that I would be sitting here now at my desk beginning an account of my wild adventures on – and off – the famous Orient Express. Neville, you see, had planned on leaving Stratton Castle that same afternoon but having had such a naughty taste of wicked little me he elected to stay on as our guest and sample what else I had to offer; for instance there was unfinished business with my bottom and Mr Johnson's Baby Oil to take care of – a transaction which both Neville and I were most eager to enter into and which was concluded very satisfactorily late that night.

The American remained with us at the castle for several more scandalous days and nights during which time Lord Ballington and I got to know him very well indeed. Neville was a quite extra-ordinary man; a blasé, super-wealthy cynic, a hedonist with comprehensive knowledge of the arts, a financial expert – yet he had spent almost his entire life on the American continent and hardly knew Europe at all. Whilst browsing in our library one day he came across a copy of Agatha Christie's *Murder on the Orient Express* and he became curious about that famous old train. I myself had never taken a trip on it; one slightly drunken evening we three decided that to do so would be a great idea, giving Neville a small crash course on Europe in wonderful luxury at the same time. Victor elected not to come. I was to be accompanied by my chubby, delightful, AC/DC maid and personal companion Matilda and of course, as always, my faithful chauffeur-cum-bodyguard – the man who had rescued me from so many dangerous situations in the past – Gregory. Neville said he would bring along one of his most stunning and sexually adventurous girlfriends; a high old time would be had by all. We would depart in mid-May when hopefully the early summer weather would be clement.

I was not expecting anything more than a most pleasant trip on a train with a little sex thrown in – you know what I mean – but, as so often happens when I go off somewhere I somehow succeeded in getting myself involved in deadly dangerous situations. Thank God I had the presence of mind to take Gregory along for, had I not, I would not be sitting here today thumping away on my old typewriter to bring you a story to follow up last year's Hollywood caper.*

Happily I am now reliving, as I write – a process which my regular readers will be aware invariably turns me on during all the sexy bits – everything that happened to me from Paris to Venice and back again. It is a glorious June day, sunshine is streaming hotly through my study window – and

* Frannie Goes to Hollywood

I am not ashamed to reveal to you that I sit here quite naked.

Uh-oh! Naughty Victor has just crept stealthily in on me. His hands, as I type, have cupped my titties, bringing a delicious shiver to my spine. He has on a thin cotton bathrobe through which – I can see from the corner of my eye – protrudes a most powerful hard-on. Gosh, he must have been turning himself on in the Blue Room again!

Nothing for it but to interrupt my work for a while and play good wifey. Bet your life he's raring for a blow-job. . .

* * *

It was not Frannie's style to start at Victoria Station, be trained through Kent and then get on a cross-Channel ferry to join the Orient Express's continental version. She preferred to fly her little party to Paris in Lord Ballington's Learjet and put everybody up in the Hotel du Louvre. The plan was that she would spend the following day lazing around and shopping before picking up the train at the Gare de l'Est that evening.

Neville Duke's choice of travelling companion met them in the first-class lounge at Heathrow Airport. She had been expecting a rather special young woman but Frannie found herself stunned by her appearance. Perhaps twenty, she was tall and willowy, rather like a model but better padded in all the right places. She was a redhead; her hair, a deep, glinty burgundy, sat on her head in a tight bunch of curls, like a swimcap. She had high, slanting cheekbones, which brought to her face a Dietrich-like quality, almost luminous, busy, green eyes and large, soft, eminently kissable lips which smiled often and easily.

The girl's name was Sandra, the 'S' pronounced hard, like a 'Z', she was German, from Cologne but had lived in New York long enough to speak English with a curiously attractive American/ German accent. She was poured into a fine black leather catsuit which fitted her as scales fit a fish, an outfit designed to bring stirrings to the loins of any red-blooded male – and presumably the occasional female – who set eyes on her.

Frannie, herself dressed to turn heads – in a slinky outfit by Givenchy – trying not to gape at this vision of loveliness as they were introduced, felt as if she was standing in the girl's shadow. Emerald and pale jade eyes met and mingled during a handshake which contrived to send tingles up Frannie's arm. For once Lady Ballington's composure was shaken; this was undoubtedly one of the most beautiful, sensuous women she had ever met.

Whilst airborne on the short hop to Paris, Matilda overcame her usual terror of being suspended twenty thousand feet above terra firma sufficiently to murmur to Frannie, sitting next to her, 'My God, that gel is something else, Fran. A real sex bomb.' Her eyes, behind their bifocals, rested admiringly on Sandra who, across the aisle from them, was leafing through a copy of *Vogue*.

'I hadn't really noticed,' Frannie responded with a quiet little smile to herself.

'Balls!' Matilda grinned at her. 'You haven't

23

stopped noticing since we met.' She wetted her fleshy lips. 'You don't suppose she's. . .?'

'That she swings both ways?' Frannie interrupted. She gazed in frank speculation at the girl. 'I bloody hope so!'

Matilda clucked her tongue. 'With your luck, she does.'

Six three, and almost three feet across at the shoulders, the massive ex-SAS sergeant, Gregory, sat alone at the rear of the plane, occupying two seats. In his huge hands he loosely held a paperback novel though he was paying scant attention to its contents. He was considering life with his boss, Lady Ballington. Despite being accustomed to her adventurous ways and her wild sexual excesses he had never quite found within his slightly prudish interior the capacity to approve of them. On every trip, without exception, that he had accompanied her she had somehow managed to get herself into life-threatening situations from which he had rescued her just in the nick of time.

As Gregory's small, cynical, rather world-weary eyes travelled over the backs of the heads in the jet he absent-mindedly fingered the beeper which was clipped into the top pocket of his jacket; activated electronically when Frannie twisted an emerald in her specially designed ring it was the signal that she was in serious trouble, his call to duty. Well – he thought to himself – not this trip. A comfortable ride on the Orient Express was unlikely to offer much in the way of peril. This time out with her ladyship and Matilda was going to be a doddle all the way. . .

* * *

At Frannie's table for three in the hushed, intimate luxury of the restaurant in the over a century old Hotel du Louvre, by the time they were almost through a delicious main course of steamed fillet of sole with saffron and caviar, sex was beginning to crackle in the air like arcing electricity.

Neville Duke, in a navy blue blazer and white silk shirt with a sporty cravat, was at his witty best as he entertained two gorgeous ladies with both of whom – though not together – he had indulged in raunchy sex; as the evening progressed it soon became plain that togetherness was what he had in mind.

The women were divinely dressed. Frannie had on a stunning, black lace sheath dress handmade for her by Valentino and very low cut. A polished emerald necklace adorned her milky, slightly upwardly pushed breasts, huge, pear-shaped emeralds, matching the necklace and almost the colour of her eyes, dangled from her ears, half covered by shiny, tumbling tresses; Sandra had on a scarlet mini-dress which fitted her as closely as her leather catsuit, very high-heeled red patent leather shoes and huge gold hoop earrings. Judging by the looks constantly thrown at their table from all over the restaurant, Neville was the envy of every man in the place.

Frannie and Sandra's eyes had clashed and sparkled on one another enough times for Frannie to be almost convinced that the girl was bisexual and that she fancied her. Reasoning that

Sandra would most certainly have been laid by Neville before dinner – thus getting that reunion satisfactorily out of the way – Frannie speculated that she might now be ready for a more complicated sexual liaison. She wondered how this might be engineered; her answer came but a few minutes later.

Neville was chattering on about his exploits on the polo field when Sandra interrupted him by saying loudly, to Frannie, '*Ja*, he is a great horseman, this I know – but what is there for the great horseman to do after dinner?'

'No night riding in the middle of Paris,' Frannie pointed out.

The American produced a delighted grin which almost split his handsome face in half. His hand found Frannie's black lace knee and patted it. 'You wouldn't like to bet, would you? Sure there is.'

Sandra's eyes wandered suggestively from his face to Frannie's and back again. 'But on horseback, no.'

Neville's other hand grasped Sandra's silk-stockinged thigh, high up, touching the hem of the mini-dress. 'How about we three have a private riding party in my suite? Undressage, perhaps?'

'I can't think what you mean,' murmured Frannie, libido churning.

Sandra, her eyes searching Frannie's with risqué frankness, huskily purred, 'If you wish you may take the long walk, Neville? Me and Frannie, *we'll* have a party,' – thus dispelling any faint doubts Frannie might still have had about her sexual inclinations.

Neville laughed. 'No way. If you dolls are going

26

to ball, here's one guy who's going to be right there on the scene.'

Highly keyed up with the anticipation of whatever the coming entanglement was going to bring, Frannie slipped off to her suite, deciding it would be fun to change from her tights into her sexiest lingerie. She was totally unprepared for the welcome which awaited her when she tapped on Neville and Sandra's door. Marching in on them at Neville's cheerful response of, 'Yeah. Hi!' shock brought her to an abrupt halt on the threshold. She gawped, the door wide open behind her. They were lounging back amongst colourful cushions on a beige velvet sofa without a stitch on between them.

Neville raised a highball glass, ice cubes tinkling. 'Maybe you should close the door before neighbours get the idea it's the Crazy Horse in here?' he said, producing his charismatic grin.

'Right,' agreed Frannie softly, barely moving her lips. 'Right.' She shut the door with exaggerated care as she fought to get her whirling brain accustomed to the situation. Her eye fell on the cardboard sign hanging over the knob. Reopening the door fractionally she hung the words 'Do Not Disturb' on the outside then locked them in, smiling to herself.

'Could be a mistake,' joked Neville. 'The last maid in here was an absolute knockout.'

'Three's company.' Frannie turned her back to the door, excitement mounting. She blatantly perused the nakedness of her companions, the opulence of the Regency style suite lost on her. 'Didn't take you two long to get out of your gear, did it?' she said. 'Like, a couple of seconds flat.'

'Neville thought we would surprise you, no?' Sandra told her.

'No?'

'So don't just stand there goggling, your ladyship. Get your sweet arse over here. Zandy'll fix you a drink.'

The American sipped from his brimming glass of bourbon and soda, propping the outside of a foot on a knee, careless of the fact – or perhaps happily aware of it – that in so doing he was making an obvious show of his genitals.

'What are you having?' asked Sandra, snaking her wonderfully lithe body to her feet, then enjoying the way that Frannie's eyes searched it in lustful appreciation as she stood waiting for an answer.

'Apart from you, you mean?' dared her not-so-ladyship as she gazed hungrily at a lush thatch of inviting pussy hair which was a similar burgundy tint to Sandra's bubble cut.

Neville chuckled. 'The famous British reserve, right?'

'I didn't get bare-arsed. You two did.' Frannie parked her behind on the edge of an armchair close to the sofa. 'I think I'd like one of those miniature Chivas Regals on the rocks.'

But vaguely aware that the music system was offering an up-tempo blues number – John Lee Hooker singing 'Good Rockin' Mama' – Frannie found herself holding her breath in admiration at the outstanding sensuality of Sandra's nude body as the girl padded to the mini-bar and dropped on one knee in front of it; she was lightly tanned all over and had a tiny waist and a back so narrow it seemed impossible it could be fronted by such large and firm breasts. As she fixed Frannie's drink down there on a white woollen rug, Sandra's raised elbows revealed that the outer curve of her breasts made them at least two inches wider than her torso. When she brought the whisky over, watching her, Frannie realised that her unblemished legs were so long that she might have been wearing high-heeled shoes. Her toenails were painted blood red to match those of her fingers and her completely flat belly played host to a delicious little, indented navel into which – apart from other tempting places – Frannie yearned to worm her tongue.

'My God, Neville, where on earth did you find such a dream of loveliness?' asked Frannie as she took her glass.

'Some scrapyard or other – I can't remember.'

'Bastard. He is one incredible bastard, no?' observed Sandra crossly. But her eyes were laughing.

Raw Chivas hitting Frannie's belly did little to calm its churning. 'Shall I perhaps get out of my gear too?' she suggested, meanwhile carefully positioning her handbag so that the cleverly disguised wide-angle lens of its concealed video camera centred, from where it stood on a side table, on the sofa.

'I have a better idea,' drawled Neville.

'Shoot,' said Frannie. The irony of the word was – perhaps fortunately – lost on the American as, reaching in her handbag for a tissue, she activated the silent camera; high-speed infra-red

29

film began to roll.

'Sandra gets off undressing beautiful broads – don't you, kid?'

'*Ja*. Perhaps I do. But you say nothing about my eyes, Frannie.'

'They're gorgeous, like the rest of you. What do you want me to say?'

'These eyes not – the ones in my bum.'

'Your *bum*?'

Neville grinned. 'She didn't notice, honey. So show her.'

The girl made a mini-production about turning around and bending at the waist to present her superbly moulded backside to Frannie. She looked at her in raunchy amusement over her shoulder as she did so. While Hooker sang ' . . . rock me all night long,' Frannie found herself staring at two deep blue, life-sized eyes in the underswell of Sandra's bottom, one on each buttock, spaced like real ones. So surprised was she that she hardly noticed the red-fringed swell of pussy lips just below them. 'Wow,' she exclaimed. She touched the tip of a finger on one. 'Are they tattoos?'

'I am not so crazy. They are transfers. You like, perhaps?'

'I – um – I guess I *like*, yes.'

'Good. I put them on especially for you.'

'Did you now?' Frannie's heart thumped. Her attention zeroed in to the provocatively framed little vulva.

'*I* put them on, but it was her idea. She's kinda coolly kinky,' said Neville.

'For you they are, yes. Shortly I think you find

out why, no?' She straightened up and turned to face Frannie, eyes burning. Her hands, fingers rigid, slid sexily over her belly until the tips of her fingers were buried in her bush. 'You enjoy to eat the pussy?'

Frannie gulped. Her loins twitched. This dream girl was something else! Glancing at Neville she saw that his cock was beginning to stir, climbing up the inside front of his thigh in tiny jerks. 'Do I have to answer that?'

'Naa. Just tuck in, baby. That is the sweetest snackbar. . .'

Sandra's horny, inviting, forward thrust of her hips as she simultaneously parted her pussy lips, was too much for Frannie to resist. She put her hands around the girl and grasped her buttocks, the ends of her little fingers hooked into the transfers, dived her nose into the softly crinkly red bush and lapped her tongue beneath it. Sandra sagged at the knees, her thighs parted and she made a little sobbing noise as she grabbed the back of Frannie's head to pull her face even tighter into her crotch. Frannie's tongue tip got shamelessly busy, flickering like the wings of a humming bird over a most delightful, small, hard nub of clitoris and then searching beyond it to find soft pussy lips and squeeze its wanton way between them.

Juices oozed; the needful German cunt tasted sweet and spicy at the same time, its natural musky smell unnecessarily complemented by a subtle perfume which Sandra had earlier dabbed on her bush. Frannie, her own pussy getting very wet indeed, savoured it with a relish most horny,

31

as if she was thrusting her tongue into a tin of the finest caviar.

'Strangely enough, such wanton behaviour kinda turns a guy on,' muttered Neville throatily, his big cock, untouched by him, steadily rising as his girlfriend clenched and jerked her buttocks while her tongue-fuck hotted up. Frannie's middle finger, watched with prurient interest by Neville, crept between the transferred eyes to find Sandra's tiny bottom hole where it slipped inside to the second knuckle to begin a vigorous jiggling. This finger and tongue sandwich activity performed on her by a beautiful young peeress whom she had fancied strongly from the first moment she clapped eyes on her so stimulated the German girl that within less than a minute her hips went rigid, her fingers screwed tightly into Frannie's hair, she grunted, '*Ja, fick, fick, fick*!', climaxed and immediately sank to her knees, Frannie's juicy tongue trailing wetly up from cunt to belly and between her breasts before their lips hotly clashed.

'Ah. You make me come so quick. Is *goot*, is *goot*,' Sandra moaned into Frannie's mouth.

Neville fisted his now fully erect cock; he began to lovingly stroke it. 'Don't stop the show for one little orgasm,' he said. 'Get her gear off, Sandra – and have yourself another one.'

With her lips mashing Frannie's, as her tongue explored the inside of her mouth, Sandra reached beneath the back of Frannie's hair, found the catch of her dress, unhooked it and eased down the zipper; when it was into the small of her back she dragged the black lace forward from her shoulders and slid it down her arms, pulling the sleeves all the way off so that the lace was bunched on her waist; her breasts, cupped underneath by the flimsiest of black silk bras, were free. Drawing the erect little nipples one at a time into her mouth she licked, sucked and nibbled them, bringing tingling shivers of delight to Frannie's spine and even more wetness to her pussy. Looking up at her with a wholly lascivious, lipstick-smeared smile, Sandra whispered, her cheeks pressed into each of Frannie's nipples. 'Lift your butt, darlink. I will get rid of the dress.'

There was almost a desperate longing in the way Frannie's hands clenched the arms of the chair as she raised her backside to allow the German girl to drag the Valentino creation over her hips, down to her ankles and off; she tossed it carelessly on to a neighbouring chair. Everything Frannie was wearing beneath it was black and of fine silk – suspender belt, stockings and the tiniest pair of knickers imaginable whose crotch was so thin and tight that a mass of her downy, light brown pubic hair was displayed around their edges.

The knickers swiftly went the way of the dress. Sandra was about to unclip a suspender when Neville, lazily masturbating, grunted, 'Why don't you have her keep that gear on, Sandra? She looks real horny in it.'

Sandra grinned crookedly at him. 'Dirty bastard. And if you want to jerk off, why you not go into the bathroom with a skin magazine?'

'Just warming up, honey.'

'Me too.' Sandra returned all her attention to

Frannie. She slid her hand slowly up from her stockinged knee and over the bare inside of her thigh top to her pussy where she slipped two fingers inside as far as they would go. 'That is some wet, wet cunnie,' she observed.

Frannie clamped her thighs on Sandra's hand and rubbed her knees together; the stocking silk whispered as Frannie breathed, 'It's *fucking* wet – and is it ever in need.'

'I see to it.' Heaving Frannie's buttocks forward to the very edge of the chair, the girl opened her thighs wide, ducked her head and put her tongue to work where Lady Ballington craved it most. Within seconds, as the tongue lewdly stabbed, Frannie gripped Sandra's ears with her thighs and entwined her fingers in her bubbly hair. Orgasm seized her. Her bottom convulsed three times, jerking Sandra's head up and down, she loudly whimpered, and was still.

Sandra looked up at her, her eyes drooping, oozing sex, her lips smeary and damp. 'Like lightning you come, you bad lady.'

Frannie grinned sloppily at her as her eyes unglazed. 'And so did you – forgotten already?'

'So was that *it*?' complained Neville. He unhanded himself; his formidable cock pointed towards them like the barrel of a miniature cannon.

'This man, he is some son-of-a-bitch, no?' Sandra's hands found Frannie's nipples and gently pinched. 'But if he wants a show, how about we give him a *show*, Frannie? We make a little *soixante neuf*?'

'Nothing could be further from my mind,'

Frannie – for whom one little orgasm was but a soupçon of pleasure to come – delightedly drawled. 'But let's do it in any case.'

Sandra climbed to her feet; her tanned knees had two white patches on them from kneeling. She took hold of Frannie's hand, helped her up and led her to the sofa where she playfully dug Neville in the ribs. 'Move over, dirty man. Make us some room and we'll boogie just for you.'

'But not for yourselves, right?' commented the American. He got up, cock swaying, and sat on the arm of the sofa.

Frannie prostrated herself on her back, head towards Neville. She eyed Sandra's burgundy-haired pussy in licentious fascination as the girl flattened her hands on either side of Frannie's thighs, dug a knee into the sofa and cocked a leg over her to straddle her breasts. Sandra eased her magnificent body carefully down, lowering her tits into her upper belly, her loins on to Frannie's face and her mouth to the pussy it had so recently satisfied. Tongues and fingers went simultaneously, eagerly, to work; Neville's hand, a mind of its own, wrapped itself determinedly around his hard-on.

This is one of Frannie's favourite sexual variations. As her tongue sinks into the now familiar cunt she suddenly understands the subtle reasons for those eye transfers on Sandra's buttocks, and why she had had Neville put them on – as she claimed – especially for her; inches away from her own, they are so lifelike they appear to be staring at her. It is weird, an added kick which encourages her in her tongue-stabbing. Her fingertips explore the eyes. As Sandra causes her to jerk her knees by sucking hard on her little clitoris as if blowing a cock, she moves her hands inwards, into the cleft in the girl's behind. An index finger finds – where a nose would have been had the eyes been real – her puckered brown hole and she eases it inside to the first knuckle.

Frannie had been too preoccupied to notice Neville leave the arm of the sofa. He is standing above her head, in his hand a smallish tin. Quietly, tensely, he says, 'A beautifully tight little bumhole, has Sandra.'

Frannie's eyes swivel to the tin and from it to Neville's heavy balls and the underside of his hard-on. Tongue dipping away, she watches as he screws the lid off the Vaseline. He holds the open tin close to her face. 'As does your arse, it needs to be thoroughly lubricated for – you know what.' He is clearly trying to control the shake in his voice. 'Will you oblige?'

Frannie is only too happy to do so. She unplugs her finger from Sandra's anus – but not her tongue from her pussy – scoops a generous amount of Vaseline from the tin with two fingers and begins to anoint Neville's target.

'And now my dick?' requests Neville.

This is strange and kinky stuff. Frannie in classic lesbian sixty-nine position, having lubricated her partner's bottom hole and now in the act of smearing grease over a rampant cock whilst she hungrily eats pussy finds this preparation for sodomy adds rolling waves to her rising tide of lust.

Neville takes the tin and puts it on the table

next to the video bag which – unbeknown to him – is recording all of this debauched activity. He gets on his haunches behind his girlfriend's backside, his knees spread and their insides touching Frannie's shoulders. With his balls resting on Frannie's forehead and the underside of his cock propped on her nose he has Frannie open Sandra's bottom hole, positions his greasy glans – and shoves.

The initial pain of this sudden buggering causes Sandra to squeal into Frannie's pussy; but her sphincter gives easily enough, the pain rapidly subsides. Enjoying the magnificently salacious pleasure of being bum-balled and eaten at the same time she responds by working two of her fingers, slippery with pussy juice, into Frannie's backside to bring to her a measure of the lusty feelings she is experiencing herself.

The AC/DC, three-way fuck machine gets into perfect harmony, each of its members gripped by somewhat different thrills; for Frannie the joy of tonguing pussy whilst being eaten and finger-fucked simultaneously is added to by the rude sight of Neville's fine cock buggering Sandra – and by the feel of his swollen balls knocking up and down against her nose as he does it; female arse-humping being one of Neville's preferred sports, he is riding an intoxicated high sharpened by the fact that his sodomitic partner is at the same time engaged in hearty sixty-nine, by Frannie's mouth which occasionally briefly leaves pussy to suck his balls and lick his plunging cock – and even by those two blue-eye transfers which he poles between; Sandra, who has nothing to feast her eyes upon beyond shadowy cunt, inner thighs and lower buttocks, is fantastically served by both prick and tongue.

The action heats up; climax approaches at a giddy pace, the music for this oddly appropriate as Dylon beats out 'Just Like a Woman'. With a final, hefty heave and an animalistic grunt, Neville begins to ejaculate in Sandra's bottom; after the initial gush he pulls his cock out to spurt over her backside and spray those eyes. Frannie and Sandra moan their orgasm into one another's pussies. Frannie's feet thump up and down on the sofa like those of a kicking baby while Sandra's fingers go rigidly still in Frannie's rear end as the nails of her other hand dig in spiteful, orgiastic frenzy into her buttock.

The sated fuck machine very slowly, luxuriously, breaks into three massively contented parts.

Bob Dylan believes it is also time for him to quit.

3

ZIPPER TRIPPER

IT WAS HARDLY SURPRISING, SINCE she had access to her husband's private jet and was chauffeured wherever she did not fly, that Frannie had not been on a train since those far-off days when she was plain, impecunious Miss Jones. Upon boarding the magnificently refurbished Orient Express at Paris's Gare de l'Est – at nine o'clock the following evening – she found herself most impressed: the train's old-world luxury was exactly in keeping with the sort of environment to which she was accustomed. Spotless, superbly furnished and decorated, it exuded a warmth most welcoming. She experienced a prickle of excitement as in her double cabin – which served as a day room until the beds were made up during the evening – she changed for dinner; in the air, she detected more than the aroma of fresh fruit and roses by her bed, of leather and polish – she seemed to smell adventure.

Passengers were encouraged to dress for dinner. Frannie was agreeably surprised as, with Matilda who was in a single sleeping compartment next to her, she joined Neville and Sandra in the diner, to find that most of the men – including Neville – were wearing black tie and many of the women had affected period-style evening dress. She had piled her hair up and had on a black, floor-length, crepe material evening gown, the high-cut bodice of which was decorated with several rows of stitched-on white pearls complemented by dangling, pearly ear-rings; to exaggerate the old fashioned touch, over one shoulder she was wearing a white, bushy fur tail.

The dining car was most elegant, its rich dark upholstery easy on the eye and the walnut woodwork, heavy-pile carpet and armed, maroon velvet-covered chairs a perfect match beneath discreet, tulip-shaped light fittings. The table-cloths were crisp, cream linen, the cutlery of finest silver, the crystal glassware beautifully etched with the Orient Express motif; Frannie felt completely at home.

'We won't actually see the French countryside,' Frannie told Neville as a first course of escalope of fois gras sautéed in muscat wine was served them. ' . . . but this part of it isn't that spectacular. The daytime travel, I understand, is reserved for the most scenically beautiful countryside – and that begins in Switzerland early tomorrow morning.' Neville was in a window seat opposite Frannie: the train was trundling through subur-ban Paris and a seemingly endless, slowly changing panorama of twinkling lights.

'Thank God no more dreadful silver bird,' Matilda commented. She squinted through her bifocals at the evening vista. 'What a remarkably civilised way to travel, Fran.' She sampled a forkful of foie gras and her slightly chubby, pleasant face broke into a beam of pure pleasure. 'Bloody good,' she pronounced. '*Bloody* good!' Her eye, in it a mixture of envy and covetousness, fell on Sandra who was wearing a sequinned, peach, low-cut dress and a matching, twenties-style headband. 'And as for the company – terrific!'

As they were leaving the lights of Paris behind and the express picked up speed through the Ile de France countryside a latecomer joined a tall, slinky-looking coloured lady who had been sitting alone, steadily quaffing white wine. He sat down diagonally opposite Frannie, facing her, and his remarkably handsome appearance arrested her attention. About forty, broad shouldered, he was wearing an immaculately tailored white evening jacket with a black silk pocket handkerchief and a wing-collared dress shirt with a floppy black silk bow tie. He had a large, squarish, swarthy face in which coal-black, wide-apart eyes sparkled as he laughed with his companion. His hair was thick, black, slicked straight back on his head like an advert for Brylcreem and he had a deep cleft in his chin. Covertly studying the man, Frannie thought that he might have been one of those gorgeous male models who so often turned out to be gay, but for the fact that his features exhibited too much character. She found it difficult to drag her eyes from him. It was inevitable that he should notice her interest in him; three times his eyes caught hers and when this happened she looked away hurriedly with a knot in her throat.

Lady Ballington found herself once again in the

41

sort of situation in which she revelled; here she was, sitting at an intimate dinner table, speeding through France with her companion, maid and occasional lover and an extremely attractive couple with whom she had indulged in wildly lubricious sex – whilst meanwhile experiencing a case of the galloping hots for a nearby male whom she had not even met.

The next time she glanced up – from a main course of beef tournedos and marrow – a thrill ran through her as she discovered that he was staring at her with such intensity that those coally eyes seemed to pierce into hers. Confused, she lowered her eyes; however, being Frannie, she pulled herself together and very quickly, boldly, looked at him again. Their eyes locked and, as occasionally – but, unhappily, rarely – occurs, a sexual message, utterly frank, totally obvious, telegraphed between them. He smiled; Frannie smiled back.

What followed was so incredible as to be almost beyond belief – something beyond even Lady Ballington's considerable experience. The man summoned a waiter, asked him for pen and paper, scribbled a note, folded it, and sent it to Frannie. Frannie opened it up, aware that Matilda was reading it with her and that the negress was staring over her shoulder at her with an interested smile on her face. It read, 'I detect in you the signs of an adventuress. Am I right? In a moment I shall leave my table. I challenge you to follow me.'

Frannie crumpled up the piece of paper and dropped it in a silver ashtray. She pursed her lips as she mustered the courage to look at the man once more. Dare, she did – and on his handsome face she discovered there was no longer even the hint of a smile; his thin lower lip was curling slightly, almost sardonically, a fine eyebrow was raised high, his expression was one huge question mark. With his eyes trapping Frannie's, he pushed back his chair and stood. Then he broke visual contact and walked unhurriedly past her table.

Frannie was invaded by a most peculiar feeling; she felt almost as if she was under some sort of hypnotic spell. She mumbled, 'Excuse me, Matilda,' and got uncertainly to her feet.

'You're not – I mean you aren't really . . .?' stammered Matilda as she slid her chair away from the table to make room for Frannie to pass.

Frannie uttered nothing more. Overcome by an incredible rush of excitement, she followed the broad, white-coated, male back through the dining car.

They made their way along the corridors of three steadily rocking, pleasantly clattering carriages; the man never once glanced over his shoulder yet Frannie was somehow certain that he knew she was behind him. They passed the door of her own cabin, then two more, and he stopped. Still without a look behind him he took a key from his pocket, fitted it into the gleaming, brass-fronted lock and opened the door. Finally he acknowledged Frannie's presence by standing to one side and silently making a gesture that she should precede him into the cabin.

She hesitated for only two or three heartbeats.

Then, trembling, tingling yet numb, wondering if she had perhaps gone raving mad – all at the same time – she stepped into the lush little sleeping car. It was much like her own except for the fact that the top bunk had been pulled down and both beds made, their linen and that of the inviting, fluffy pillows a light, warm ochre.

She heard the door close behind her as she stood, swaying with the motion of the train, looking dumbly through a window into the speeding night. There was the metallic click of a bolt being shot into place, the sound falling on her ears much louder than it actually was. Her throat constricted; she swallowed hard. She tried to come to terms with the fact that she was locked in a cabin, alone, and presumably about to be made love to, by a stranger who had turned her on simply by the way he looked, by his eyes, and with one short, dynamite-charged note. Her nerves twanged, her heart thumped like a hammer trying to break out from within.

'I . . .' she stuttered, ' . . . we don't even . . .', she began to turn her head, 'I don't even know your . . .', strong, confident hands grasped her narrow waist; the simple contact made her gasp, 'I . . . name,' she finished, in a whisper.

His breath was merely warm, but it seemed to scorch the back of her neck as his lips closed in to kiss it below her swept-up hair. He kissed, he blew lightly, he nibbled, he trailed his mouth wetly around and up until it was just below her ear; had her eyes not been screwed closed she would have seen her earring dangling on his nose. His hands crept forward to meet on her belly and then began to slither upwards as he nibbled her earlobe and thrust the tip of his tongue in her ear; the restless, searching hands cupped her breasts and squeezed.

Frannie was as weak as a newborn foal; she felt dizzy, close to fainting. Yet something nagged in her mind, insisting she should make some sort of protest; by allowing a complete stranger to use her in this fashion she was behaving like the most brazen of sluts.

'At least tell me your name?' she blurted out, voice weak and shaky. As she made a half-hearted attempt to dislodge his plundering – and enormously arousing – hands she rolled her head and opened her eyes on the darkness beyond the window, vaguely noticing a sliver of moon.

Still he uttered not one word. His lips returned to the nape of her neck, kissing their way up to the other ear as he unhanded her breasts and grasped her wrists. His groin was poking into and rubbing against her backside, the hardness there making her shudder. Acting as if any argument from her was out of the question – and thus rendering it so – he shoved her forwards to the window, lifted her arms above her head and had her take hold of the shiny brass curtain rail. She was desperate for him to say something – anything at all, just so that she could hear his voice – but he did not and the protracted silence as the train rumbled on somehow added an odd spice to the horniness of her situation.

His hands dropped again to crush the pearl-encrusted crepe around her breasts. The express entered a tunnel and she was suddenly faced with a sharp reflection as the hands slipped down over her belly until their fingers came together in a vee to scrunch the skirt material into her crotch.

Mewling, almost unbearably aware of the wetness of her pussy and its extreme need, she tightened her grip on the curtain rail until the knuckles whitened and bit her bottom lip nearly hard enough to draw blood, as the train emerged from the tunnel and clusters of lights appeared, not far from the tracks, as it approached the town of Meaux.

The lust-arousing rummaging at Frannie's loins was brief. The man's next action was swift and certain – and it brought her to the very pinnacle of lewdness. Getting on one knee behind her he clasped her ankles beneath the hem of her dress and ran his hands without pause all the way up her silk-stockinged legs and bare thigh tops to her silken, Bonni Keller-knickered bottom, hooked his thumbs on either side into the waistband of the panties and dragged them down to her feet, over one black patent, spiky-heeled shoe to leave them hanging loose around the other ankle. Her cheek sagged into the backs of her hands, eyes once again closing as she waited – prepared, eager, to accept anything this dominant, macho male was about to do to her; she felt breathless.

Briefly, he left her. She was aware of the sound of cupboard doors as they opened with a faint squeak. Then he was back and his hands were prizing hers from the rail. He spun her to face him. His arms wrapped around her, his lips locked on hers, his tongue forced its way into her mouth. She responded with an enthusiasm bordering on the rapacious, grinding her crotch against his silk-trousered hard-on and sucking his tongue as his fingers on her bottom gathered the thin, black skirt material handful by handful until the hem was bunched into his fists, and her backside, naked, starkly white, was clearly exposed for anyone who happened to be watching the express as it slowed down amongst the houses which now bordered the tracks.

He turned her around and, tongue on the rampage in her mouth, walked her backwards four paces. The heap of dress became imprisoned against her lower back by his wrists as his hands slipped under her buttocks and he lifted her a few inches to deposit her bottom on something cold, smooth and hard; he had sat her on a wash-basin between its open, Sapelli pearl inlay doors which had first been installed more than sixty years previously. His hands left her behind; the back of the dress unscrunched to pile itself over the basin.

The stranger's black eyes seared through hers all the way to her libido as, holding the stomach-churning gaze he stooped, grabbed the front hem of the skirt and hiked it up, bunching it at her loins, the bottom of her pussy on display just beneath it. Both of Frannie's hands were on his shoulders; she was watching his actions with eyes so glazed with lust they might have been those of a drunk. Removing one of her hands he coaxed her to hold the dress material high on her belly with it and spread her thighs so that she was fully exposed to him. His eyes smouldered on her pussy. Swiftly unzipping his fly he put his hand inside, pulled white mini-slips down over his genitals and hauled into view a darkish, throbbing pole of a cock.

Frannie pants with desire and makes tiny noises which sound as if she is begging – which, indeed, she is – as the man takes first one leg, then the other, and hooks her feet over his shoulders. Positioning his cockhead, he holds it nestled between her pussy lips for agonising seconds then, as her eyes widen on the tantalising sight and she flattens her dress against her belly so as not to block the view, he crams his cock all the way up inside her until their pubic bushes – his an intriguing contrast to hers in its utter blackness – mingle and his balls are dangling against the marble front of the basin.

Her hands are linked around the back of his neck. He disengages them so that, cock unmoving inside her except for its throbbing pulse, he can remove the white fur tail from her shoulder, unzip her dress and pull down its bodice.

Frannie impaled to his balls by a silent stranger – a gorgeous hunk of masculinity who has so far deigned to utter not a single word – on an antique wash-basin on the Orient Express with one of her most expensive evening dresses in a wrecked heap at her waist, her bare tits gently juddering with the motion of the train, her dangling pearl earrings swinging, the backs of her silk-stockinged and frilly suspendered thighs flattened into the man's beautifully cut, white dinner jacket, her calves on its shoulder. Yet another masturbatory fantasy has become wonderful reality!

He withdraws his thick prick to the glans, holds it there so that they can both drink in the sight of cojoining cock and pussy, plunges to the hilt again – eliciting a little squeal of pleasure from Frannie – and sets about steadily, energetically poling her. The train meanwhile goes slower and slower.

Frannie – on a trip to Paradise with this rutting stranger – achieves her first orgasm, jerking her naked bottom on the cold of the sink as it rips through her. She pants, running her tongue tip over her teeth. She calms, happily settling in – as the cock bangs in and out of her – to what she knows is going to continue to be a truly ribald fuck experience.

She craves to see more male flesh. With her bare back pressed into the gilded mirror she reaches for his belt and, not without difficulty since he is slamming it into her like a stud at a mare on heat, unbuckles it and unbuttons his trouser top. Of their own accord, encouraged by his violent movements, the slippery trousers drop to the man's ankles. Frannie pulls aside his shirt tails to afford herself a fine view of a muscular, hairy belly. She lifts the crumpled front of her skirt from where it has obscured the sight of their locked genitals. Then she reaches for his bouncing balls, latches on to them and squeezes. He grunts loudly, the very first sound he has made. His hands grip her tits harder, thumbs and fingers pinching her erect nipples. Frannie's fingers stray to his jerking arse, digging into it. His balls slap into the marble as his fucking – incredibly – becomes even more furious. She comes again, with a little shout.

The faster the screwing, the slower the train. It

has reached Meaux station where a number of people are awaiting the next train for Chateau Thierry. It does not stop, but it passes through at little more than a walking pace. Frannie's fingers are lodged in the crack of the man's taut and pounding behind as she notices, around the side of his shoulder, lights, a station platform, people. There are several astounded looks, but she is too far gone in this amazing fuck to care; perversely, she grins.

The express gathers speed as does the rutting of the man, who has reached the point of no return. As it is leaving the station his backside gives three massive, climatic heaves and his semen surges forth. Feeling its heat and wetness within her, Frannie hits the high spot herself. Her eyes are rooted on their genitals as the heavily erupting cock is yanked out of her to shoot over the insides of her thighs, her pussy and her belly. His face is contorted, his eyes pig on his soiling as its effect on Frannie is to heighten her final orgasm to such a pitch that she loudly screams; the sound is drowned by a long, piercing whistle from the train.

The man sagged into Frannie, his breathing harsh and heavy, perspiration streaking his face, his wilting, dripping cock crushed into the front of the wash-basin. Frannie's eyes closed, her hands went limp, one trailing against his thigh, the other palm uppermost over her saturated pussy, her skirt tumbling across it. Her breathing slowly relaxed as her heart ceased to sledge-hammer.

She experienced a lethargic repletion and not

the slightest shame while she marvelled at the extremes of telegraphed need which had brought about such an extraordinary, wonderful fuck. Recovering, the man lifted her legs down from his shoulders and, as she opened her eyes, handed her a small towel; he wiped himself with another.

'Uh – you do have a voice don't you? And presumably a name?' she ventured, dabbing his sperm from her pussy.

'Sure,' he said, grinning his easy, hypnotic grin. He dropped the towel, bent down, pulled up his trousers, adjusted his underpants, tucked his shirt in and closed his zipper.

She waited for him, whilst cleaning her belly and her thighs, to volunteer information about himself, but he said nothing. As he finished buckling his belt he was watching her wiping herself, his eyes leering and a twisted smile on his face. She got rid of a final splash of sperm which left its stain on her stocking top then stuck the towel behind her. 'Well?' she insisted. 'Just who the hell are you? I mean one really ought to know. After all, we *have* just. . .'

'My name is Angelo Salamini. I am Italian, Lady Ballington,' he said.

She sharply drew in her breath. 'Then you know my name?' she said, staring surprise at him. 'How is that possible?' She heaved herself off the wash basin and began putting her dress back where its maker had meant it to be; the crepe, she noted in relief, had stood up well – it was barely crumpled.

'Stratton Castle? A garden party? Early summer last year?'

She hiked up the front of her dress, eyes searching his face. Now she remembered. 'Then you must be *Prince* Salamini?' It had been a fleeting introduction; someone else had been very much on her mind at the time.

'Indeed I am. But – to my chagrin – you hardly noticed me. You were being very heavy with an American movie star. Chester Becker I believe his name is.'

She slicked closed her zipper. Of course, she had been utterly involved with the famous star; she had to have been to have ignored this Italian macho. 'Well,' she said, eyes running seductively over him as she reached for his crotch and treated his genitals to a goodbye squeeze. 'I seem to have noticed you now, don't I, my prince?'

4

BUNK BONKS

FRANNIE WAS ALMOST UNCOMFORTABLY AWARE of the glances which came her way as she made her way back through the dining car – this time with Prince Salamini behind her. Ridiculously, she was harbouring the idea that people must be realising what she had been up to with the man.

Having read the note and knowing her mistress only too well, Matilda goggled in amusement as she made room for Frannie to retake her seat; she even had the temerity to mutter, as she brushed past her, 'Zipper fuck, was it?'

Mouthing the flattest of smiles at her, slight irritation in her eyes, Frannie sat down. Their companions made no comment, but they seemed to be studying her questioningly; glancing at her watch she saw that she had only been away some fifteen minutes – rather a long time perhaps for a visit to the loo but equally a remarkably short time in which to have indulged in sexual intercourse with a stranger. She wriggled her behind on the chair. It felt slightly squidgy; a little of Angelo Salamini's sperm was leaking out of her and its effect was to make her feel deliciously dirty.

Her prince, she observed, was holding his dusky beauty's eyes and speaking quietly to her whilst the woman threw several barely surreptitious looks of interest in her direction. Frannie reasoned – correctly – that he was describing the experience to her.

Outside, the lights of the outlying houses of Meaux drifted away and all became blackness; even the thin slice of moon was hiding behind cloud. The train was at full throttle, the regular muted thunking of its wheels speeding along the tracks a pleasantly relaxing sound. Salamini ended his bodice-ripping narrative and both he and his girlfriend smiled knowingly in Frannie's direction; with a toss of her head she smiled unselfconsciously back.

'New friend, then?' commented Neville Duke, noticing.

'You might say that, yes.' Frannie savoured a mouthful of wine. It was a particularly delicious Chateauneuf du Pape which slid down her throat silkily. On Matilda's instructions the remains of her main course had been cleared away just before her return but she had in any case lost her appetite.

'I'd swear I'd seen him before,' said Matilda, surveying the prince through the top half of her bifocals as a sweet of Summer Fruit Charlotte was served.

'You have.' Frannie reminded her of last year's riotous garden party at the ancestral castle.

'When you threw a wobbly over Chester Becker. Right.' She glanced at Salamini again. 'He's every bit as gorgeous as Chester, I'd say.'

'And as talented,' Frannie confided in a giggled whisper in her ear.

'Did you say Chester Becker? *The* Chester Becker?' asked Sandra, who was getting slightly the worse for drink.

'She did,' Frannie told her as she toyed with her fruit.

'You are knowing this man, Frannie?'

'I am, I am.'

'This is the small world, no? Me, too. Two years ago, Chester and me we, you know. . .?'

'Got it together?' Frannie finished for her.

'Been around, has our Zandy,' said Neville, squeezing her thigh. 'Well-travelled young lady.'

Frannie chuckled. 'How curious. We appear to be sharing the same men.'

'Lucky sods,' said Matilda. She again let her gaze wander to Prince Salamini and was rewarded by a friendly smile which prompted her to remove her spectacles. She now saw the world through a haze but at that moment, in close proximity to two handsome men, she preferred that to looking – as she considered she did with her glasses on – unattractive.

'Why don't you get contact lenses, Matilda?' asked Neville, taking proper notice of her for the first time. His eyes strayed to her large melon-sized breasts which seemed to be making a determined effort to burst out of her low-cut, emerald-green velvet neckline.

Unable to see the look of sexual interest which would have gladdened her heart, she told him, 'Bloody nuisance. Too damned finicky. In any case, they make my eyes sore.'

After dinner Sandra was feeling a little unwell from the combined effects of too much wine and travel. She retired. The other three moved into the sophisticated comfort of the bar where a pianist was playing a baby grand. It happened that the only room for them was in a seating area already partially occupied by Prince Salamini and his girlfriend, and they joined them.

The dusky beauty was Yvette, she was French. Her black eyes sparkled on Frannie in amused curiosity; she was evidently intrigued that her beau had pulled off the amazing feat of seducing this lovely English lady during dinner – and most keen to discover what sort of woman it was who would indulge in a quickie on a train with a stranger.

The party had settled in, drink flowed, the conversation was trivial, friendly, the grey-haired, jovial pianist – Simon Becker – tinkering around with 'Just One of Those Things' when Frannie asked, 'How on earth did they get that piano on the train?' It was more than half as wide as the carriage itself.

'I assume they had to remove a section of the roof,' Salamini told them. 'But they don't say. It's one of their best-kept secrets.' He seemed to know a great deal about the Orient Express, he travelled on it often. He explained how the original train of legend had not been one train at all but dozens of privately owned sleeping and dining carriages which were constantly interchanged and plied several different routes. The present express, he said, was made up of carriages which had survived the war and subsequent disuse; it had been refurbished to the last luxurious detail and was presently in its fourteenth year of service.

As the evening drew late Frannie, pleasantly

light headed, found herself in an ever more intimate huddle with Angelo and his Yvette whilst Neville Duke – to the surprise of Frannie and delight of Matilda – was paying flirtatious attention to Matilda.

The inevitable happened. 'I can hardly ask you back to our cabin a second time without Yvette joining us,' Prince Salamini suddenly said.

Yvette smiled sexily at him. 'Eet would not be very polite to leave me alone in zee bar,' she murmured. Her slender, mauve-nailed hand fell on his thigh. 'Besides, you do to me like you promised? Please?'

He stroked the back of her hand as he quietly asked Frannie, 'Do you perhaps like girls?'

Frannie swallowed. Her eyes travelled in obvious interest over Yvette. 'Take a guess.'

'You like girls.' Glancing around the bar quickly to make sure no one was watching him, he cupped Yvette's breast as he said, 'Of course I will keep my promise. But with one small variation. *We* do it to you, okay?'

'Okay. Yes, please. Then – we go?' she started to get to her feet.

'We go.'

Keyed up with excitement, wondering what sexual variation was in store this time, Frannie followed the negress's lithe, sensuous back out of the bar. Behind her, Angelo lightly fingered Frannie's buttocks.

'The party seems to have split up,' observed Neville. 'Sandra's sick – so that seems to leave just you and me, Matilda honey.' His hand found her thigh.

Matilda's heart was thumping. She could hardly believe her luck. It had been a long time since she had been in anybody's arms but Frannie's – and the previous gentleman had been bordering on the elderly though far from lacking in enthusiasm. She dared to touch the young American's thigh-invading hand as she stared in what she hoped was her most sexy manner at his blurred features. 'My place, then?' she muttered.

He laughed. 'My God – are you as fast as Frannie?'

'Steady on – you *are* talking about my mistress, you know.'

'In how many ways – mistress, I mean?'

She raised an eyebrow at him as she squeezed his lean hand, 'That'd be telling, wouldn't it?'

'I just bet it would.' He grinned, then he said, 'Frannie seems to be just about as fast as this train.'

'And as well travelled.'

'Not to say even better upholstered.' He stood, taking her hand. Even though she could but vaguely make them out, his eyes contrived to make her shiver with the suggestive way they wandered over her curves. 'But then, so are you.'

She became bolder. 'And you, I take it, would like a closer look?'

'Hell, yes.' He pulled her to her feet. 'Your place, then.'

Matilda had forgotten the fact that she had neglected to completely unpack her suitcase; there it sat, where she had left it, open on the floor, partially tucked under the little, polished walnut bedside table with its crystal carafe of water and red-shaded brass lamp. It seemed fate that the American's eyes should fall on it as she was locking the door on them. 'What on earth?' he asked as, insides a bundle of nerves, she turned to face him. She followed his gaze; amongst some scrunched items of smalls – mostly prim white cotton, but one or two rather more frivolous pieces – lay a black rubber dildo of impressive dimensions. Matilda could barely make it out, but she was most painfully aware that it was there.

'Oh, um, well never *mind* that,' she stammered, embarrassed, as she dropped hastily to one knee and dragged a petticoat over the object.

'But I find it most intriguing.'

She lamely tried to stop him, but he was quickly on his knees beside her and rummaging for the dildo. He held it up, whistling in admiration. At least nine inches long, fat, exquisitely moulded to the distended veins down its back, the sculptured glans and a bulging pair of testicles, it had attached to it some fine velvet straps.

'I, uh, take it you don't use this alone?' he asked. 'I mean, it's not a vibrator as such, is it?'

Matilda's cheeks had turned a bright shade of pink. He was holding the dildo close enough to her face for her to be able to make out its features in all their gross glory. 'That's hardly your business.'

He shrugged, 'I guess not. But here we are, together, alone, intent on sex and. . .'

'But not with *Othello*, for Heavens sake!' she blurted out, instantly regretting it.

He roared with laughter. 'Is that what you call it? Kinda figures.'

Defeated, Matilda looked sheep's eyes at him. 'It's what Frannie christened it.'

'Ah. Then you and she. . .?'

'Not often. Sometimes.'

'Boy, would I dig seeing that.'

'Wouldn't you just. All men are dirty bastards.'

'It's your damn dildo!' he protested.

She smiled. The embarrassment had been fleeting. Now, seeing the dildo in the hand of a man she had brought to her cabin for sex gave her vivid memories of her last session with it with Frannie; her hots for Neville increased.

'Why don't you put it on?'

'*What?*'

'I just have an irrepressible urge to see you wearing friend Othello.' He thrust his face close to hers, so close that his handsome black eyes with their dark, curly lashes, were in sharp focus. She found herself overpowered by the man and by her need for sex with him. His lips met hers, his tongue probed – as at the same time he slipped the dildo inside the low front of her dress between her fat tits and rolled them together over it.

He broke the kiss. 'Why don't you stand up?' he muttered, breath hot on her cheek. 'Let me strap it on for you?' Pulling the dildo from her cleavage, as he squeezed a breast with one hand he ran the other down to her groin and pressed the artificial cock between her legs. 'No?' he grated. 'Or yes?'

Matilda began to feel very raunchy indeed;

some dirty little games prior to the main event, she decided, would be most welcome. She struggled to her feet, muttering 'Why not?'

'Pull your dress up.' His voice had thickened.

Looking down into the blur of his black-curled head, feeling tremendously horny, Matilda did Neville's bidding without hesitation. She scrambled the skirt of the heavy, ankle-length evening dress up until it lay rucked in a heap beneath her forearm at her waist. She was wearing green tinted stockings held up by flesh-coloured suspenders, and a pair of fine-mesh white knickers through which her heavy bush pushed darkly. Plump thighs bulged, startlingly white, above the stocking tops.

'I do love a meaty woman,' rasped the American. He swayed forward to bury his mouth in Matilda's fleshy, yielding pussy. Whilst blowing hot breath through the knickers he slowly pulled them down until his lips were in direct contact with her naked bush. Then, with Matilda gasping and her knees trembling in over-eager reaction, he moved his mouth off her to fold the knickers down her thighs. He examined the dildo. 'Let's see how this incredible thing works,' he muttered. 'What's this funny shaped bit behind the balls?'

'It's, it's to excite the woman who's wearing it.' The words spilled hesitantly from Matilda's lips, falling strangely on her ears almost as if they were coming from someone else's mouth. Her lewd exposure was bringing her most feverish delights.

'Is it now? They thought of everything, didn't they?' He untangled the straps and put Othello in place. 'Hold it there and turn around.'

Matilda did so, bawdy feelings coursing through her. Neville busied himself taking a strap between her legs and two more around her waist then buckling them together. He sat back on his heels, eyes lusting on the fat, white buttocks so appealingly divided by a thin, mauve velvet strap. Briefly, he mauled them, pulling them apart to uncover Matilda's bottom hole – no stranger to a penis. He pressed and rolled them together – they felt much the same as had her tits. Then he turned her around. Had Matilda been black the monstrous rubber phallus with her heavy bush realistically topping it would have appeared remarkably real; as it was, it presented a picture of most grotesque ribaldry.

'Jesus,' breathed Neville. 'And you really fuck Frannie with that?'

'And she sometimes fucks me.'

'Jesus.'

For some reason Matilda whimpered.

'And if I move it like, *this* . . .' – he took hold of the dildo and gave it several small and rapid jerks as if wanking it – ' . . . it does things to you?' He jerked it harder. '*Right*?'

'Owwww!' Matilda's eyes closed. Her knees sagged.

'It does things to you.' But he stopped. 'Strip everything off, honey. I'm just raring to sample the full delights of those Michelangelo curves.'

Her eyes opened droopily. Poutily smiling, she crossed her hands over the rucked-up skirt front and pulled it up, over her head and off to drop it on the bed. Her huge, braless tits shuddered violently then settled down to wobbling with the motion of the train. 'Rubens,' she muttered.

'How's that?'

'The pink, chubby ladies – they were Rubens, not Michelangelo.' She was feeling incredibly lewd, utterly bawdy. Behind the dildo her partially plugged pussy was oozing and tingling. Seizing Othello she did with it what Neville had, plump white fingers masturbating the huge black cock and with it herself.

'Yeah. You *do* that while I climb out of my gear,' breathed Neville, his flesh and blood cock, hard as rock, straining beneath his trousers.

Matilda could not restrain the vulgarity spilling from trembling lips. 'You want for me to hump your bum?' she asked.

He had removed his jacket. He went very still, holding it trailing on the floor in one hand, shaking his head. 'You and Frannie,' he muttered. 'You and Frannie. Jeeessuuuus!' Dropping the jacket he opened his zipper. 'Thanks anyway, honey, but gay I ain't!'

* * *

In Prince Salamini's cabin, Frannie was leaning with her back to the corridor door and sipping champagne from a fluted crystal tulip glass. She was thoroughly engrossed in the arousing sight of the nubile Yvette unashamedly, enthusiastically naked on her back on the lower bunk as Salamini stripped her skimpy knickers off her feet and stuffed them into his jacket pocket. He glanced up at Frannie as he ran an exploratory hand over the girl's smallish, taut breasts. 'Yvette has the most delightful body, would you not agree, Frannie?' he asked.

'Sensational,' she breathed. 'Indeed, nude Yvette – her smooth, ebony skin in pleasing contrast to the honey-yellow satin sheets of the bed – presented a most erotic picture; her delicate nipples were lightest brown, the hairs of her humpy pubis a tight clutch of crinkly black whilst those of her head hung in a mass of dreadlocks, interwoven with colourful beads, over her thin shoulders. Frannie, very happily tipsy, mind filled with the memories of what had occurred to her so recently here in this cabin, was once again hotly randy – and more than ready for whatever was to take place now.

Yvette, stretching her body luxuriously, running a hand suggestively from breast to crotch, muttered, 'You do to me now what you 'ave promised, *n'est-ce pas*?'

'I never break a promise.' The prince's hand slithered down over her flat little tummy with its lovely, indented navel, to trace its way over a thin line of hairs leading from navel to pussy thatch where it slid under her own, neatly manicured fingers playing amongst the springy pubes. He again looked at Frannie. 'Would you please let me have your stockings?' he asked her.

'My *stockings*?' Frannie echoed, puzzled.

'As I recall you're wearing pale silk stockings? Could I have them?' he repeated, stretching his hand from Yvette's pussy towards Frannie.

'All – all right.' She downed the rest of her champagne and put the glass on a small varnished walnut trolley top where it joined company with a large bunch of purple grapes – and her video bag. Kicking off her shoes she hiked first one side of her dress then the other to unclip and roll off her stockings, keenly aware that the prince's attention during those moments was no longer on naked Yvette but on her own legs. She handed him the stockings, then, as he looked back at Yvette, slightly unsubtle about it because of her bellyful of liquor – but fortunately unnoticed – she opened the bag and set its camera in motion.

'Kneel and face me, sweetheart,' Angelo instructed Yvette. She obeyed with unseemly eagerness, her head slightly bowed because its top touched the underside of the upper bunk, her dreadlocked hair hanging over her breasts. Taking one of her hands he secured it with a stocking to one of the upper bunk's metal supports, then tied the other to the opposite support so that her arms were stretched broadly above her shoulders in a similar attitude to that of hanging from a cross. Cupping his hands just above her knees, he splayed her legs, then he stood back to gloat at her; her dusky thighs were so slender that they displayed interesting dents starting halfway up their insides and widening into her crotch. Her wiry bush was thick and black between them, red pussy lips protruding through the hairs.

'She is a little perverted,' Salamini mumbled. 'She really enjoys this sort of thing,' he told Frannie, without taking his eyes from the girl's pussy.

'Evidently,' said Frannie, wetting her lip; her own pussy was beginning to crave more action.

The prince mumbled something in Yvette's ear

and her droopy, chocolate eyes, smouldering sex, swivelled to Frannie's, catching them, holding them, bringing a little knot to Frannie's stomach; for the first time, Lady Ballington, glad of it, realised with certainty that the negress was thoroughly bisexual. Her full lips trembling, Yvette whispered, '*Oui.*'

Angelo once again held out a hand towards Frannie. He asked her politely for her knickers.

'My *knickers*? Well, *okay*,' she responded. She fished her hands up beneath her skirt, hooked her thumbs in the waistband of her panties, stripped them off and gave them to him.

He inspected them with a lecherous smirk. 'Damp, of course, from earlier,' he commented. 'That's great – because Yvette loves the taste of pussy juice. Don't you, my pet?'

The girl's little grunt of agreement was smothered as Angelo stretched the silk Bonni Keller knickers around her lower face, pulled their crotch between Yvette's lips and knotted them behind her head.

The little scene, serenaded by the soothing, regular thunking of steel wheels against track joins and steadily rocked by the train, was becoming increasingly more kinky. 'Now what happens?' Frannie murmured hopefully, a hand scrunching her dress material between her legs to tease her pussy. 'Are you going to beat her?'

'Not at all. We're going to treat her to a tongue bath.' He licked his lips. 'How's your mouth – is it dry?'

'Not while there's plenty of bubbly.'

'Good. We drink champagne and meanwhile

we mingle our saliva all over her tits, her belly, her thighs – and of course her cunt. But first we get naked. You approve of the idea?'

'Absolutely not. It's wicked. It's bloody depraved!' The shake in her voice was caused half by the alcohol and half by sexual tension. She was already dragging her dress over her head.

Watching her with a goatish eye, Angelo said, as he peeled off his jacket, 'We strip nude and then we make her wait. Perhaps we'll finish another bottle of champagne first. We, ah, we *toy* with one another's bodies, feeling, kissing, – get her unbearably worked up by watching us. Let her wallow in the joys of her bondage before we excite her even further with our tongues.'

Unzipping his trousers, the prince stepped out of them and then his briefs. A solid erection poled through his shirt front; he took hold of it, lewdly waving it at Frannie. 'Agreed?'

'You, er, you got yourself a deal.'

She stripped off her final bits and pieces. Taking her cue, delighted to have been thrown into yet another of those carnal adventures in which she so revelled, Frannie dropped to her knees. 'Let's work up a thirst for more bubbly, then,' she said, thickly. She closed her mouth over the princely prick.

* * *

Whilst Frannie had been sipping champagne as she watched Salamini divest his French fuck of her clothes, a few cabins away a sudden priapic wildness had overwhelmed Neville Duke. For a long time his sexual companions had been on the slender, or at least only slightly buxom, side; presented with a naked female of the ample proportions of Matilda, a lusciously chubby heap of flesh whose wobbly tits were crowned with big, erect, pink nipples and whose black forest of pubic hairs was cushioned between bulging white belly and strapping thighs – a woman, moreover, who was jiggling a huge, black dildo protruding from her crotch to titillate her pussy as he undressed in front of her – he was virtually exploding with lust. As soon as he was naked he had leapt on this vision with a primitive growl, shoving her backwards to the bed and heaving her down on to it. Not bothering with its buckles he had wrenched the dildo down her legs and off as if it were a pair of obstructive knickers, clambered on top of the gasping Matilda, roughly spread her fat thighs and rammed his throbbing cock into her to the hilt.

Now, as, close by, Frannie on her knees gives Angelo Salamini enthusiastic head, Neville, humping her maid with all his plentiful energy, finds his mind crammed with licentious ideas. He regains a certain amount of control. The heaving of his buttocks calms down. He grunts salacious words in Matilda's ear: 'You like butt fucking?' he asks her.

'But fucking what?' gurgles Matilda, misunder-standing.

For an answer he withdraws his cock to the glans, stills it and creeps a hand under her bottom and between its cheeks. 'Would you like *this* . . .' he grunts, then jams his cock home to his balls, making her squeak and shudder, ' . . . in *there*?' and he pokes his forefinger past its second knuckle into her anus.

'God,' she goes, 'Oh, God, *yes!*'

Pulling out of her he heaves himself off her and stands. He grasps her by the thighs and twists her around, bringing her knees down to the heavy carpet pile so that she is doubled over the bunk. Cradling her cheek on her hand, impatient for the unnatural penetration, she bites her lip as her other hand steals beneath her flattened tummy to find her pussy and she squints over her shoulder to try and see what he is doing in her misty field of vision. She can make out little, but she hears the sound of running water as Neville wets a cake of Imperial Leather at the wash-basin. Seconds later she is squirming and wriggling her bottom as first the soap cake is rubbed between its cheeks then two very slippery fingers are thrust inside her anus and twisted and turned.

There is a dull thunk as the soap drops from Neville's trembling fingers to the carpet. Holding her breath, anticipating what for her is a rare, but exquisite pleasure, Matilda feels rough hands greedily grasping her buttocks to stretch them wide. The unmistakable sensation of the head of a cock thrusting at her sphincter causes her to squeal into the back of her hand and to bite its skin.

Matilda's bottom hole submits to its breaching with little trouble; there is a brief moment's discomfort, no real pain and – only with effort managing to control himself from ramming his hungry cock all the way home – Neville achieves his buggery step by slow and easy step until his balls are cushioned in two mounds of trembling buttock flesh and all he can see of his genital area is his mass of pubic hair comfortably nestling across the crack of Matilda's arse.

All ten of the American's fingernails claw the soft skin of his target. Words – all but incoherent – tumble from his slack, spittle-flecked lips. 'So fucking tight, *so* tight,' – Matilda understands – ' . . . like the cunt of a virgin.' The salacious words serve to further excite her; she jams two fingers into her soaking pussy to the third knuckles and fantasises that she is in a two-prick sandwich.

Handsome face made fiercely ugly with rampant lust, dark eyes pigging, black curls flopping down in disarray over a sweat-streaked forehead, Neville gets completely into the swing of his sodomy while Matilda almost swoons away with the exquisitely dirty sensations the supposedly illicit act brings to her; she feels as if her bowels are on fire. Her vagina goes through a series of violent contractions on her fingers and she comes, howling her rush of animal gratification into the satin sheet.

Neville is in no condition to hold back for long; he has never screwed so plump an arse before and the sight and feel of his cock driving between the luscious white orbs – which wobble like vast jellies beneath his raking hands with each raunchy thrust – quickly brings him past the sexual point of no return.

Wallowing in the voluptuous aftermath of massive orgasm, her fingers unmoving inside her, Matilda is only vaguely aware of the accelerated pumping of the prick in her bottom – she is equally as conscious of the vibrations of the train through her knees on the carpet – but Neville's strangled shout as he begins to shoot brings her heightened awareness; as his semen begins to flood her back passage she awakens to this new sensation of wicked delight and by the time the final drops drain into her she is gasping with the thrill of it.

Performing a clumsy sort of flopping roll, the temporarily exhausted and satiated American contrived himself on to the floor, his back against the bunk and one arm crooked over a pillow. His head lolled on a shoulder, his eyes were closed, he was perspiring and breathing heavily. Matilda, bottom hole feeling deliciously stretched, pussy twitching, folded her legs beneath herself on the carpet next to him. Narrowing her eyes into slits – bringing the man as near into focus as she was able without her spectacles – she surveyed his powerful, naked body; in particular, the wilting cock which was leaking sperm amongst the hairs of his thigh. 'My gosh,' she muttered happily to herself. 'My *gosh*.'

Matilda could not remember ever having had a sexual experience with quite such an impressive specimen of manhood. She reached out a prurient hand to cradle the fine set of genitals, wondering if Neville would be capable of getting it up once more on this marvellously wanton evening; she found herself hoping desperately that he would.

* * *

71

Frannie was back on the wash-basin for the second time that evening – rather, to be more precise, she was on Angelo Salamini who was perched on it with his long and princely legs straight out in front of him and Frannie squatting on his lap, her back to him, her thighs splayed across his thighs, her pink-painted toes on the floor, her hands on her knees and with his hard-on lodged very comfortably all the way up her aristocratic pussy. As, while his hands made free with her tits, fingers and thumbs rolling around her nipples, she steadily rode him – more or less in time to the clattering rumble of the train wheels – her tipsily lusty eyes were rooted on the trussed and gagged Yvette.

The French negress was close enough to the rutting couple that if Frannie stretched out a hand she would have been able to touch her. Gaze latched on Frannie's bouncing pussy and Angelo's poling cock and trembling, hairy balls, Yvette was swinging gently on her tethered arms with the express's motion whilst jerking her crotch in a needful fucking movement, the slender muscles in the inside tops of her thighs contracting and relaxing as if by this effort alone she could bring herself to orgasm.

The girl's show of libidinous excitation, her erotic demonstration of sexual appetite bordering on desperation, her subjugated state, plus Frannie's own exhibitionism – how she adored to be watched whilst being fucked! – all contrived to fill Lady Ballington's loins with such craving for relief that she suddenly broke her regular screwing rhythm, her hips jerking wildly as if she were on a bumpy, galloping horse. Mewling, hair flying around her face as her head rolled with her exertion, she came with a shudder which went all the way down from her shoulders to her curling toes. She went quite still, glazed expression fixed between her legs on Salamini's cock as an inch or so of its damp base continued to appear then disappear inside her; the prince, well in control of this kinky scene largely of his own engineering, was saving his sperm for the sweetly tortured Yvette.

Angelo's buttocks ceased their heaving. With his fingers locked together beneath Frannie's tits he nuzzled her neck below her ear and whispered, the tickle of his breath bringing her out of her lethargy. 'When you are quite ready, randy lady, it will be time for Yvette's spit bath.'

Cocking a leg, Frannie climbs off Angelo, his rock-solid cock making a faint squelching sound as it slips out of her, its wet head trailing across her departing thigh. She picks up the half-full champagne bottle – their second – puts its neck to her lips and, in most unladylike fashion, upends the bottle and drinks thirstily. Then she hands the champagne to Angelo and mutters, 'Why don't you lead the way?'

He retains his dignity – as far as a naked man with a glistening erection is able – and pours champagne into a glass before sipping it, for the prince's blood – unlike that of Frannie who merely married her title – is truly blue. Then he says, 'Come.'

Together they kneel, side by side, in front of Yvette, faces almost touching her fine little tits with their hard, pink nipples. 'We take a breast each then we work our way down to her belly,' mutters Salamini eagerly. 'We make her truly wet.'

Filling her mouth with saliva, Frannie soaks her tongue and licks all over Yvette's right breast as Angelo does the left; the negress's tit is very firm and tastes faintly salty. Their tongues meet in the cleft of her bosom where they briefly mingle, then they trace their wetly salacious ways down her torso to come together once again at her belly button as Yvette whimpers into Frannie's gagging knickers and sensually wriggles. They arrive at her wiry pussy hair, begin to lick it then the prince insists their mouths away.

Yvette's ebony flesh gleams in its coating of spittle, heightening Frannie's desire to tongue her pussy; but Angelo has other ideas.

'I'll see to her little rabbit,' he tells her.

'Rabbit?'

'Since she fucks like one.'

'And what are you going to call mine?'

He hooks his fingers into her pussy and rocks them there. 'Yours? *This*? How about cunt? Precious cunt.'

She shudders. 'Original.'

'Get yourself behind her and lick her bottom. Properly. All the way over. And don't forget the crack. *Deep* in the crack.' His voice now sounds as if he is beginning to strangle.

Frannie scrambles on to the edge of the bed on her knees and crawls behind Yvette. Once more she fills her mouth with saliva – there seems to be no shortage of it for this arousing task – and goes eagerly to work lapping the superb, taut buttocks, spreading her spit evenly over the delicious mounds. The black bottom is never for one second still, it is impossible for the French girl to keep it from frantically jerking because of the exquisitely horny sensations the two mouths are bringing her.

Saving her pussy until last, Angelo thoroughly salivates the inner tops of Yvette's thighs. Finally his tongue tip eases its way into its tasty prize at the same moment as Frannie's, having soaked her buttock cleft, finds her tiny bottom hole to work its wet way inside.

Yvette is now producing loud, continuous grunts. She heaves her pelvis with such furious abandon that her lovers are obliged to cling tightly to her hips and keep their faces pressed into her in order to maintain tongue contact with her most intimate parts.

Her cheek squashed into Yvette's writhing buttock, Frannie slides it to its underswell, trailing her tongue down from the girl's well-teased and wetted bumhole and along her perineum until, her nose crushed against the sweet smelling sweaty underside of her bottom, her tongue finds her cunt where it meets Angelo's, cramming in there with it.

The mutual pussy eating is brief; Yvette bangs her hips with such fervour that both tongues lose contact.

'Enough,' rasps Salamini. 'I'll see to her now.' He stands, grasping Yvette firmly by the waist, struggling with her, finally managing to almost still her. 'Put my dick in, Frannie,' he grates.

With the prince flattened against Yvette's shiningly spittled torso and clasping her tightly to him, Frannie reaches between the ebony thighs, fists his cock and puts the glans between the girl's red pussy lips. In one powerful thrust Angelo's big cock is all the way up the negress and his balls are cupped in Frannie's restless hand. 'Take your knickers off, Frannie,' he gasps.

For a second she fails to understand – her knickers have long since been off – but then she does and she reaches up to free Yvette's mouth. The girl loudly moans. As Angelo's cock relentlessly pounds her pussy the moan rises to a shriek and finally a climactic scream. Her entire body goes rigid, then, just as quickly, limp. With a grunt bordering on the savage, Prince Salamini yanks his cock out of her to direct his erupting semen over her belly, her crotch and her thighs.

A hand tense on Yvette's hip, Frannie peers around the girl's sagging body to watch Salamini's milky come splashing and mingling with drying spittle on the gorgeous black flesh. The drained prince sinks slowly to his knees on the steadily vibrating, throbbing floor of the cabin.

Aroused beyond endurance, Frannie lies on her back, her head cushioned by down-filled satin, closes her eyes and begins to masturbate to what is destined to be a swift and devastating climax.

*　*　*

In Matilda's sleeping car something stirred; it was fat, warmish, soft and silken and for fifteen minutes or thereabouts while its proud owner took a well-deserved rest it had lain unmoving in Matilda's cosseting palm. Now, it twitched to life as Neville Duke's long-lashed eyes flickered open. Lazily, he grinned at his crotch.

'Frightened I might sleepwalk, were you?' he asked her.

She moved her face very close to his and blinked his swarthily handsome features into clear focus.

'Wouldn't want to lose you, not just yet.' She treated him to an affectionate penile squeeze which was rewarded with faint signs of growth.

His eyes swept appreciatively over nude, chubby flesh. 'Just like your mistress, aren't you?'

She chuckled dirtily. 'I'd make two of her.'

Taking hold of her breasts from beneath, he lifted them; like two great, white, water-filled balloons they drooped over his hands, engulfing them. 'Twice as much fun, then.'

'I doubt that.' She glanced down at herself with a slight grimace. 'There's altogether too much of me.'

'But I enjoy the occasional wallow in curvy, yielding, female flesh. You can have enough of the skinny model variety.'

'Can you? *I* certainly can't.'

He laughed at her. 'You Brits are amazing.'

'We like variety. At least, Fran and I do.' Her hand moved from his cock to cradle his balls as he played with her tits, rolling them against one another. A voluptuous shiver went through her. 'She gets almost all the action. I seldom seem to have enough.'

'You mean you don't fuck all her men friends?'

'Almost never.' It was true. 'They normally hardly seem to notice me.'

'Beats me why.'

'Come on. It's bloody obvious. She has all the glamour, all the money and sex appeal in the world.'

'You resent that, do you?'

She shot him a look of genuinely hurt surprise. 'What makes you think that? Of course not – I adore her.'

'Sorry. Glad to know it.'

She lifted her hand with its heavy load of male genitalia, testing, as though she were weighing it; his cock had failed to live up to the promise of its recent tremble. 'I betcha if Frannie happened to be handling you like this right now you'd be all the way up.'

'That doesn't necessarily figure. Not if I'd just thrown a heavy fuck into her as I just did into you.'

She raised an admonishing eyebrow. 'I *beg* your pardon?'

He chuckled. 'The language? My Bronx upbringing. It has the habit of sometimes showing through.'

'I bet you're a self-made man.'

'Right on. And I've always known what was best for me, what I needed to do next. Like, right now . . .' he paused, looking at her speculatively.

'Yes?'

One hand left a breast to take hold of his cock and jiggle it. 'You want this up again, am I right?'

'Maybe.'

'You want it up and there's one way to get it up

very quickly.'

'Suck it?'

'That too. But it wasn't what I had in mind.' Rolling away from her he stretched out a hand for his trousers and slipped their black crocodile belt from its loops, then doubled its end and buckle together.

Matilda's eyes widened. 'An American with the English vice?'

'You don't own an exclusive on it.'

She licked her full lips, trying to focus clearly on the belt, failing. 'Do I beat you, or do you beat me?' she asked, already beginning to tremble in anticipation of a sport which she invariably enjoyed.

'Both.' He handed her the belt, and stood – to bend over and support himself on his hands on the bed. 'You me first.'

Matilda's vanity flew out of the window into the speeding French night. Needing to be able to measure her distance – and craving, besides, to feast her eyes with clarity on what she was about to do – she found her handbag, fumbled in it and took out her bifocals. With them perched on her nose Neville and his naked backside and dangling cock and balls were suddenly alarmingly distinct – and the desire to treat the luridly proffered part of his anatomy to the thrashing he had requested overwhelmed her. 'How hard?' she asked with shaky voice, raising the belt on high.

'I'll let you know if it's too much. Just hit me.' His words were clipped short, betraying his rising inner tension.

Matilda brought the crocodile hide down in a

sweeping arc to slap it across the American's buttocks. It wasn't powerful enough a blow by any means and she knew it, but she wanted to hear it from his lips.

'Harder,' he growled.

Crack.

'Harder. Much harder.'

Crack!

'More, bitch. *More.*'

Crack!

Getting massive, wicked enjoyment from her actions, Matilda feels her pussy ozzing as she lashes the reddening, hairy male arse. Each time the belt – which is only, after all, lightweight and incapable of inflicting serious damage – bites into buttock flesh, Neville emits a loud pleasure grunt and Matilda sighs. She pauses between swipes to peer in prurient curiosity around and below his thigh; as she hopes and suspects, his heavy cock is all the way up and pointing straight ahead beneath his firm belly.

More blows, enthusiastically delivered. A violent passion seizes the American. Growling like some angry, wild beast, he straightens up, grabs Matilda's belt arm, wrenches the belt from her hand, twists the arm behind her back and forces her, gasping, to her dimpled knees.

'I'll teach you, you fucking *bitch*,' he snarls. 'I'll teach you to do this to *me*!' Aware that this show of anger is par for the course in such a play-sadism scene, she happily tenses her behind for what she expects will be a powerful blow.

The belt falls, fuelled by the strength of his lust, with a sound like a pistol shot. Matilda's fat behind shudders; an instant, livid welt appears across both buttocks. A second, whipping slap connects, then another and another in swift, stinging succession to paint distinct red stripes across one another as the shaking, abused cheeks turn cherry red and Matilda squeaks and squeals, head cradled in the crook of her arm on the edge of the bed, balls of an index and second finger passionately jiggling on her clitoris.

Matilda, like Neville before her, is positively revelling in this smarting, tolerable pain. As the strip of dead crocodile lashes on she is visited by fleeting memories of the last occasion when – far too long ago – she had been similarly chastised.* It had been in a moonlit forest glade with a switch – complete with leaves – broken from a rhododendron bush and was administered in front of a crowd of devil worshippers by a massive negro called Cossi who had afterwards sodomised her in front of the entire assembly, including Frannie.

With this event mistily in her mind – and as belt stripes her for perhaps the twentieth time – Matilda climaxes with a wail and sags into the bed.

But this is not quite the end. Neville whacks her twice more, falls to his knees behind her, thrusts his throbbing prick into her pussy and commences to fuck her with such animal energy – his balls swinging and slapping into the backs of her wobbling thighs, his fingers pinching a nipple, a thumb digging to its base into her rectum – that

* *Frannie Rides Again*

by the time his second load of the evening gushes into her she comes right along with him, her shout muffled by the sheet into which her face is pressed; Matilda has enjoyed one of the most exhilarating sexual romps of her life.

Meanwhile, Frannie, the insatiable Lady Ballington, beautiful mistress of Stratton Castle, undisputed queen of the Wiltshire country set, is locked mouth to pussy on the lower bunk of Prince Salamini's sleeping cabin with the gorgeous French nympho, Yvette, while the distinguished Italian prince, having earlier clambered up on to the upper bunk in order to sleep, is raunchily watching their lesbian couplings from there, head lolling over the edge of the bed, eyes smouldering and with his commendable cock – to even his own surprise – growing once more.

Oblivious to the highly lubricious activities within its elegant, venerable 'sleeping' compartments, the luxurious Orient Express thunders on its way towards the Swiss border and the historic town of Basel.

5

ROOM WITH A PHEW!

WEARILY CONTENT, SEXUALLY REPLETE, FRANNIE stuffed her knickers, stockings and suspender belt into her handbag and began to pull her dress over her head. Prince Salamini, having achieved the not-inconsiderable, agreeable feat of fucking both her and Yvette yet again, hauled himself for the second time to the upper bunk – this time with the absolute intention of snatching some sleep. Yawningly, he said, 'I have some business in Zurich. I shall be getting off there and staying for a few days.'

Frannie dragged her dress on, Salamini tiredly watching her body disappear. 'What time do we get there?' she asked.

Yvette, on her tummy, enticing rump humping under a sheet, softly snored.

'Six thirty in the morning. Why don't you join me?'

Frannie gaped at him, bleary eyed. 'You've got to be kidding. I have to sleep. Besides, I've booked the entire trip straight through.'

'People get on and off the train all the time. You can change your booking whenever you like.' He yawned again, very heavily, talking through it as Yvette grumbled a dream. 'I own a suite in the Imperial Hotel in Zurich. You can catch up on your sleep there in the morning – they were going to wake you early for breakfast in any case.'

She ran her fingers through her hair, unsuccessfully trying to straighten its post-coital mess. 'God, I don't know. I shall have to disturb my entire party.'

'They can stay on the express. You can take a plane and catch up with them later.'

'I never go anywhere without my maid and chauffeur.'

'I can put them up in the hotel.' His eyes seemed to clear. They travelled in little, piercing jerks over her evening dress. 'Besides, we have unfinished business.'

Frannie was tempted. But she was mildly stubborn. 'We do?' she said. 'No – you do. Banks, is it?'

He ignored the question. Eyes melting away her dress, he told her, 'I have a very special room in my suite. A sex room. I would very much like for us to enjoy it together later.'

Which, naturally, was the clincher for Frannie – and was how she came, fearsomely tired, clad in designer jeans and a thin apricot sweater, to be rapping on the door of Matilda's sleeping car at five-thirty in the morning.

When, after knocking several times, she managed to raise her, Matilda, a sheet wrapped around herself, opened her door only fractionally. She squinted myopically through the gap.

'For God's sake let me in,' grumbled Frannie.

'Shit. All right – if you insist.'

The large, naked frame of Neville Duke was huddled into the partition wall on the far side of the room's single bunk. Neville was firmly in the land of Nod.

'Oh,' said Frannie, somewhat taken aback. Her eyes swept over the familiar figure. 'Oh!' she went again.

'He, um, *we*, um . . . well. . .'

'You certainly did, didn't you?' Frannie noticed almost simultaneously the crocodile belt on the floor and the redness of Duke's buttocks; she picked up the belt. 'And just why would he remove his belt from its trouser loops?' she asked, a wicked smile creasing her face.

'I guess he, ah, he. . .'

'Show me, Matilda.'

'Now, *Fran* . . . ' Matilda was now well and truly awake. She backed away as Frannie reached for her body-draping sheet.

Laughing, Frannie insisted, '*Show* me!' She made a lunge for the sheet and dragged it off her, ducking behind Matilda as she attempted to back herself against the wash-basin. Frannie whistled. 'Impressive.' She laid a hand on the crimson, striped behind; it was hot to the touch. 'You dirty, perverted cow. And with *my* guest!'

Matilda actually blushed the same colour as her buttocks. 'You're not going to be angry with me, are you?'

A short explosion of mirth from her ladyship. She put her hands on Matilda's shoulders and planted a delighted kiss on her cheek. 'Don't be bloody daft. Jealous, maybe.' She eyed Neville Duke and his red backside. 'Wake him up.'

'But it's almost six in the morning.'

'And we're leaving at half past. Wake him.'

'*Leaving*? Whatever for?'

'We're getting off at Zurich.'

'But why?'

'Never mind.' Frannie raised her chin towards Duke. 'Wake him.'

Matilda took hold of the American's broad shoulders and shook him gently. When there was no response she did it more roughly. He grunted and rolled towards her on to his back. Then he snored. Matilda shook him again; he was proving almost as difficult to wake as a man dead.

'Pull his whatsit,' suggested Frannie, with a mischievous grin. 'Give it a good tug.'

Giggling, Matilda followed instructions, grabbing his penis and yanking on it, at the same time bending close to his ear and shouting for him to wake up. That did the trick. First one eye opened, then the other. Reaching for his assaulted cock, Neville grumbled, '*Heh*. What the hell?'

"Morning, lover,' said Frannie. 'Strayed into the wrong bed, did we?'

His eyes clearing, he pushed Matilda's hand away and propped himself on one elbow. 'Frannie! Well, *hi*! C'm'ere!' he said with a grin.

She smiled. 'Some other time. We're about to leave the train. You should get dressed.'

He glanced at his gold watch. 'You must be nuts. I'm a clean-living American boy. I need my beauty sleep.'

'Suit yourself. We're leaving the train.'

* * *

Flughafen Station, Zurich, six forty-five a.m. on a slightly chilly, unwelcoming morning. Figures of weariness, Frannie and Matilda, Yvette and

Angelo Salamini emerge from the splendid portals into a greyly filtering dawn light. They are followed by a chirrupy Gregory who, annoyingly, feels – in his own words – bright as a daisy, and accompanies a porter with an electric trolley heaped with their luggage.

Fleeting impressions from Frannie's early-morning-muddled mind: a silver grey, 500 SL Mercedes elegantly in wait for them outside the imposingly grand station, black chauffeur – in an immaculate uniform matching in colour the paintwork of the car – in obsequious attendance; tall, slender streetlamps, their yellowish light in losing battle with the dawn; passing with only the faintest of clatter as it whispers away from the station, a tram, modern, clean lined, impossibly spotless by British public transport standards; a street-sweeping machine with gleaming blue and white paintwork whooshing along surrounded by a fine mist of water; few people; the glittering foyer of the Imperial Hotel, unreal at that time of morning; a beautiful, Regency-period furnished bedroom; a silken-sheeted double bed; carelessly peeling off her clothes to strew them over the Persian carpeted floor; bed; instant, dreamless sleep.

Matilda and Lady Ballington refreshed, bright-eyed, clear skinned and with not the slightest indication of their strenuous sexual romps of the previous night in their demeanours, were tucking into a hearty brunch at twelve thirty when Matilda remarked, 'Jolly threesome, was it?'

'Thought you had one yourself?' said Frannie, archly, through a mouthful of crispy bacon.

'What are you talking about?'

'You, Neville Duke and a crocodile. Well, an adaptable piece of crocodile hide.'

'Very funny.'

'Sore, are you, today?'

Matilda wriggled as she sipped her tea. 'Hah!'

'I noticed from the colour of his bum that you did it to him, too. Whupped him, I mean.'

'So what if I did? But I do believe I was asking about you, my love.'

'Me? Oh, you know. . .' she shrugged and prettily smiled, the perfect picture of virginal innocence, ' . . . the usual usual.'

'I wonder who *he* is?'

'Who?' Frannie's eyes followed the direction of the four of Matilda to alight on a hulk of a man who was taking a seat at an otherwise empty table. 'Gosh,' she said, impressed.

He had long blond hair, thin and slightly streaky, looking as if it had been bleached by the sun; it was tied into a bushy pony tail with a thin red silk band. His face was large-featured, craggily handsome, bronzed, with a very faintly lop-sided look about it and a determined chin. But, above all, it was the eyes which grabbed; smallish, deep-set beneath thick, blond brows, they were of the palest watercolour blue, like iceberg ice just below the surface on a bright summer day.

'Dead tasty,' muttered her ladyship, as her inspection moved from his face to an immaculate, satiny, charcoal-coloured suit and a neat cream silk shirt with a colourful tie.

'I should have thought you had quite enough

on your plate.' Matilda cut a careful slice from her grilled tomato and popped it into her mouth.

Frannie raised an eyebrow. 'Never get too much, you should know that.' Her attention strayed from the man. 'How's Gregory?'

'Uncomplaining for a change. Describes this trip as a doddle.'

'Let's hope it stays that way.'

'It's been terrific so far.' Her eyes shone.

'Has it not?' agreed Frannie. Drily, she added, 'But unhappily for you Mister Whiplash stayed on the train.'

'You have to remind me?'

The bronzed giant nodded to them when they went out; Frannie responded with a formally polite little smile.

They took themselves shopping in the smugly self-satisfied centre of Zurich where the people and the elegant white-stone buildings were as immaculate as the neat tram-lined streets – and where scarcely a cigarette butt was to be seen littering the ground, never mind anything as insidious as a discarded ice cream or sweet wrapper. There was an almost hushed formality about the bustling city as if international banking was the world's most respectable business and the purveying of wildly expensive watches more vital to life than the sale of bread; in one wide thoroughfare alone, behind a dozen or so squeaky-clean shop windows there must have been on display tens of millions of dollars worth of watches. In this same street austere, important-looking buildings played host to institutions such as Bank Leu, Union des Banques Suisses and

Schweizerische Kreditanstalt, and Swiss national flags with their white crosses displayed against a red background, abounded like poppies on Poppy Day.

Arm in arm, Matilda and Frannie wandered curiously through the broad portals of the mighty Swiss Bank Corporation where there unfolded an odd little scene which typified the Swiss national character; in a vast, dome-ceilinged banking hall Matilda uncased her camera and prepared to take a picture. A security man – so expensively and smartly dressed he might have been mistaken for the manager – slid to her side.

'Pardon me, madam,' said the man, quietly but firmly, recognising the Englishness of the miscreant, ' . . . I am afraid it is strictly forbidden to take photographs within the confines of the bank.'

'Oh. I'm so sorry.' Chastened, Matilda lowered her Praktica.

'That is perfectly all right, you were not to know,' the man went on with a grave and grey smile. He even offered an explanation. 'It is not that we would object to having pictures taken of our beautiful building, but we are obliged to respect entirely the privacy of our clients.'

'Quite so,' breathed Frannie, offering him her friendliest smile.

Back in the street, Frannie remarked, 'Extraordinarily polite people. Had that happened almost anywhere else in the world the man would almost certainly have acted hostilely.'

Matilda laughed. 'England for example. "Oi – put that bleedin' camera away. Don't you know the effing rules? Can't you bloody read?" '

'And there *was* a warning sign in there. A very clear one in three languages.'

When, laden with packages, in the middle of the afternoon they returned to the hotel, Prince Salamini was occupying a table where they could not fail to miss him, where an open-plan bar area merged with the foyer. As they approached him he stood to greet them, folding his *Wall Street Journal* and inviting them for a drink.

It was the first time that Frannie had seen the prince since retiring that morning and as they idly chatted about her and Matilda's little shopping expedition her mind became crowded with impressions of her raunchy night together with the man and Yvette.

The black girl appeared but just as quickly left without taking a drink; it seemed to Frannie that there had been an unspoken signal between her and Salamini but Frannie made no comment about it. Almost as if he was divining what was going on in her mind as, fancying him, she was renoticing how appealingly handsome he was, how deep the cleft in his noble chin, how his slicked back, shining black hair perfectly suited him, taking her hand he got to his feet.

'I have something I should now like you to see,' he said, tugging Frannie's hand. As she stood he told Matilda, 'Drink whatever you like – it's on my bill.'

They left her sitting with the little pile of parcels. In the lift, their ascending companions a typically correct, ageing Swiss couple in expensive but dowdy clothes, taking Frannie in his arms Angelo asked her, his voice pitched at

91

normal level, 'How do you feel about sex in the afternoon?'

She noticed the man's eyebrows shoot up as the woman frowned. The lift stopped and the couple got out, the woman whispering something to the man in Swiss German and glancing furtively over her shoulder at Frannie as the doors closed.

She giggled. 'You did that deliberately.'

'Bunch of stuffed shirts,' he said, pulling her close to him and rolling his crotch against hers. 'It amuses me to shock them whenever I get the chance.' His hand dropped to her calf and crawled up over her tights beneath her loose, knee-length beige jersey wool dress until it found her buttocks and squeezed. 'Well?' he whispered in her ear.

She shivered. 'Well what?'

'Making love? In the afternoon?' He pulled the back of her pantihose, together with her knickers, down to bare her bottom and two of his fingers found their way between her pussy lips from behind, making her gasp.

'Any time if it's with you,' she muttered hoarsely as the fingers slipped deeper inside her. 'Your sex room, no?'

'My sex room – yes.'

Its immediate impression was one of discreet opulence; then, before Frannie had a chance to take in her shafting sunlit surroundings, Salamini pressed a button and they dramatically changed.

Heavy, maroon velvet curtains swooshed closed as low, ingenious lighting softly infiltrated the room, complemented by the soothing sound of Schubert. 'Sit. Enjoy,' said the prince. He led her to an eastern gold and silver silk upholstered couch. As she sunk into the welcoming softness of one corner her eyes darted around. Angelo perched on the edge of the couch next to her and gentled her breast.

The room was furnished with a mixture of Indian and Arab styles, the floor covered with a magnificent Chinese carpet scattered with colourful rugs. It was spacious without being enormous, wonderfully comfortable. Frannie's eyes alit on one of three, life-sized, white marble statues which were very slowly and silently revolving on their plinths. It was most elegant, not kitsch but a pornographic work of art; a naked man and woman, their entwined forms draped in white light from a small ceiling spot – and therefore the more startling – were engaged in sexual congress. The woman's feet were off the floor and wrapped around the backs of the man's sturdy calves. He was supporting her with both hands beneath her buttocks and leaning slightly backwards; as her bottom, inch by inch, turned towards Frannie his genitals came clearly into view. A thick penis was poled three quarter of its length into her; below it hung a heavy, perfectly sculpted scrotum.

Frannie's attention shifted to the second statue – a girl on her knees, very young and with small tits, fellating a beautiful young man – then on to the third in which the most powerfully muscular of the masculine figures had a sinewy woman supported lengthwise down his body, her thighs wrapped around his face and her feet crossed at the ankles above his head as they indulged in a standing sixty-nine.

'Golly,' Frannie breathed appreciatively, eyes wide.

'You like my statues?' Angelo's hand got rougher with her breast.

'I'll say.'

'I had them especially commissioned. They were vastly expensive, but well worth it, I think.'

'They were actually *modelled* for?'

He chuckled. 'Photos were. I'd dearly like to meet the man who could keep it up for weeks at a time!'

'So would I.'

He unhandled her breast and leant forward, reaching for a tiger-skin-covered coffee table on which sat a polished copper hookah pipe. With a bookmatch he lit a tobaccoey mixture in its ornamental top as he drew on a gold-thread-braided tube extending from the pipe's base; there was a bubbly sound. A sweet smell invaded Frannie's flaring nostrils as the prince exhaled smoke and handed her the ivory-stemmed mouthpiece.

'Superb marijuana,' he said. 'Columbian Gold – from Guajira where the climate for growing it is perfect.'

She felt a touch awkward, as always in similar situations. 'I'm sorry,' she told him, 'I'm not into drugs.'

He shot a look of surprise at her. 'How come? This stuff is really great for sex.'

'I've tried it, of course, but it doesn't do anything for me.' She smiled suggestively at him. 'And my sex life couldn't be better.'

'Please yourself.' He inhaled deeply, holding the smoke down for several seconds before lazily exhaling it through his nose. 'Drink something?'

'How about a little champagne? I'll knock back some bubbly while you blow your bubbles.'

'And then,' he said, as he got up and went to a fridge which was concealed behind arabesque, silvered metal latticework, ' . . . *you* can blow *me*.'

'I just might do that,' she murmured, a little lump of excitement forming in the pit of her belly.

As he unscrewed the wire at the neck of a bottle of Krug, her eyes explored the room more thoroughly. A section of it, she noticed, was a largish alcove, the ceiling of which – from what she could see of it – was intriguingly covered with small pieces of fractured pink mirror, hidden by a hinged screen of a similar latticework to that which disguised the fridge.

'What's behind the screen?' Frannie asked as she heard the champagne cork come out with a soft plop.

'That is where we shall shortly find ourselves,' he told her as he thrust a foaming glass into her hand. 'And then you will find out.'

It crossed her mind that he might have something like an S & M collection hidden away there. Well – she thought – just as long as he doesn't try going to extremes; she fingered her emerald ring, taking comfort in the knowledge that one twist of the stone would electronically summon Gregory – somewhere not too far distant in the hotel – if this Italian prince should get unduly rough.

'I take it the explicitly erotic gives you quite a

kick?' he said. He dragged more pot into his lungs, eyes roving amusedly over his statues.

'Right where it counts,' she boldly told him.

'Me too. Yet, unhappily so much porn is cold and unappetising, cheapening the performers, making something of a mockery of sex. Unattractive people not really appearing to be greatly enjoying themselves; fake attempts to make it appear as if they are – the girls smiling asininely at the camera, that sort of thing. Unpleasant, yet, even so, often arousing to the sex-starved consumer.'

Frannie who – for the sheer dirty excitement of it – had enjoyed several little forays into the world of porn over the previous few years, told him about her first experience in Florida with the proprietor of the aptly named *Prick* magazine, one David Hansom.*

'I had a great time,' she concluded. 'But nevertheless it was frustrating, being posed having sex with guys, having to keep still all the time while the cameras clicked away.'

'Most of the porn people use that technique and in my opinion it's because the photographers aren't talented enough. The models should move like in the videos and really get into it – a really top stills photographer will successfully capture the most exciting moments. I have the proof.'

Frannie blinked interest at him as she helped herself to more champagne. 'You do?'

His eyes swivelled to the screen. 'Behind there, you'll see.' The promise fell lazily on her ears, a

* *Frannie*

Columbian Gold-induced drawl.

Sexual electricity sparkled between them. Frannie regretted that she had had no opportunity to collect her video bag; the afternoon, she knew without the slightest doubt, was about to get good and steamy.

'Why don't you take off your clothes?'

Pulse quickening, she emptied the contents of the glass down her throat, watching him over its rim as she did so. Then she murmured, 'You, too?'

'Of course. I brought you here to fuck.' The words slipped out so casually he might have said, 'I brought you here to play chess,' and in so doing added to the rising sexual tension between them.

Little more than a minute later, having watched each other climbing out of their clothes they were naked, a couple of yards apart, facing one another. Angelo sported a magnificent hard-on. Frannie, gaze glued to his prick, oozed damp within her needful little pussy. She poured yet more champagne as, his glazed eyes wandering over her nude body, he stooped to take a final drag on his hookah pipe.

'Come,' he said. Taking her hand he led her to the silver filigree screen. He pulled aside one corner and took her through; the area behind it housed a two-metre-square double bed covered with a pale blue and grey Indian silk spread, itself liberally sprinkled with intricately patterned silk cushions. There was a metre of space all around the bed between it and the walls, and in the centre of each wall against a neutral silk covering was an oblong film screen. Similarly positioned at the bottom of the bed was a free-standing film screen in front of a projector box.

Angelo made himself comfortable on his back on one side of the bed, his thick erection pointing straight up. He drew Frannie down beside him and tucked a shiny red patterned cushion behind her head. 'How do you like the effect?' he asked, staring at the ceiling.

The broken pieces of pink glass were not set perfectly level with one another; they threw an interesting, if slightly confusing, fractured image of themselves at the occupants of the bed. 'Nice,' whispered Frannie.

'I wanted something different from the usual line of ceiling mirror. A little more subtlety.'

'Mmmmm.' Lady Ballington, who actually at that moment desired nothing more complicated than the potent cock by her side, witnessed her pinky sharded self enclose it in her fist.

The prince sighed comfortably. 'You get on with wanking me while I demonstrate to you what this part of the room is all about.'

There was a small control box on the floor on his side of the bed. Reaching down, he pressed some buttons; the room beyond the filigree screen went dark as at the same time a pale red glow pervaded the area of the bed. The music switched to soft jazz – Stan Getz playing 'All God's Chillun Got Rhythm'. The screens glowed life. On the screen facing them at the foot of the bed, in subtle colours – somewhere down the scale towards sepia – appeared the photographed image of an extremely pretty girl with tumbling red tresses. Facing the camera, she was propped amongst cushions on a cane sofa, her knees drawn up and her hands crossed on the fleshy insides of her thighs, their brown-tinted nails framing her naked, ginger-pubed pussy. She was wearing a plain white suspender belt, flesh-coloured stockings and a white slip disarranged to display one smallish breast with a delicate pink, uptilted nipple. On her lovely face with its wide-spaced, auburn eyes and full-lipped, slightly drooping mouth was an expression most attractively wanton, sex in very line. She had no need to be given words for her to be saying, unmistakably, 'Come here. Enjoy.'

Frannie glanced at the other three screens; all displayed the identical picture. Angelo, more intent on his erotic pin-up than on Frannie's lazily cock-pumping fist, murmured, 'Meet Belinda. I selected her from more than one hundred hopefuls.'

'You commissioned her personally?'

'I set out to do a better job than the porn kings. I believe I succeeded – but you'll be the judge. I stage-managed everything, right down to the make-up, choosing only performers who were renowned for revelling in their work. And do you know why stills, rather than video?' He looked at her, putting his hand over her masturbating one, stopping it.

'Tell me.' His hard-on seemed to be growing hotter in her fist.

'Because I have so often found myself freezing frames when watching porn videos. I like to spend time with what I find are the best moments. The rest, I find, soon becomes boringly repetitious. So I put together for myself, with the help of two of the most talented photographers in the world, a series of fantastically horny stills.' He reached towards the floor. 'I'll put the machine on automatic. It lingers on each picture, as you will see, long enough to absorb every lascivious detail before moving on.' He pressed another button then coaxed Frannie into renewed cock fisting.

The delightful Belinda changed position. She was now sitting up, knees raised and pressed together but her feet splayed to present a salacious view of her pussy as, lips slightly parted, she admired herself in a hand-held, gold-framed mirror. A swarthily handsome man in a striped cotton shirt was looking down on her from behind the cane sofa, face radiating desire.

'Mikhail,' commented Angelo. 'One of the most sought-after, reliable performers in the porn business. A randy stallion if ever there was one. And a most remarkable stayer.'

Frannie was intrigued by the superb presentation and beginning to be woozily swamped with libidinous desire. As she tossed Angelo she cupped her free hand under his bulging balls and lustfully squeezed.

But he still seemed to be more interested in his pictures than her ministering hand. He told her, as the scene changed, 'The reason for four screens is that when making love each of us, in whatever position, is presented with the same image. Togetherness.'

A superb close-up appeared; head and shoulders only, Mikhail on the sofa with Belinda, licking her neck; her face raised, her mouth open, both their eyes closed. No sex organs, yet a masterful study of imminent sex.

As the famous Getz tenor bopped whisperingly along in the background, the outer door of the room silently opened and closed. Yvette, nude and melting into the dark, only the shining whites of her eyes evident, padded to a chair and sank down into its cosseting softness; from it she had a perfect view of the bed through the slightly displaced screen. As she made herself comfortable she watched Salamini's hand find Frannie's pussy and the masturbation becoming mutual.

Superbly erotic porn surrounds the bed; Mikhail, wearing only his shirt, legs open, robust prick – thick as Belinda's slender wrist – in the girl's hand as they passionately kiss; her eyes drooping, exuding sex, Belinda savours Mikhail's glans with her tongue tip; in the next shot his legs are spread while, swooped over him she licks his balls, sparkling pendant earrings dangling, hair awry, his knee perched on her thigh, his hand tucked under a suspender, three probing fingers at her plumpish, curly-haired pussy lips. Not the slightest self-conscious awareness of the camera with these two – they are lovers, alone, lost in one another's splendid bodies.

Taking hold of Frannie's loose hair – which was in as attractive a disarray as that of the porn girl – Angelo tugged her head down his body to coax her mouth over his cock. As she avidly sucked he lifted her hips from the bed and twisted her around on top of him as easily as if he were playing with a baby. He examined the glorious pussy nestling between milky thighs spread on either side of his hairy chest, he licked it, he opened the vulva with both thumbs, his tongue plunged. With his nose crammed into the crack of Frannie's behind, the prince still had a limited view of his pictures.

Frannie, head bobbing, watched the screen at the foot of the bed, where ... a close-up of genitals and hands. Belinda's legs in the air – you can see the smooth, inside backs of her thighs, the swell of the bottom of her buttocks. Mikhail stands in front of her, only his mid-section on camera, a hand – framed by the open cuff of his striped shirt – clutches his cock at the base, fingers curled into his balls; his other hand, wrist hooked around Belinda's thigh, is spread over her pubic bush and his index finger and thumb have opened her pink pussy lips. Fractionally below her hard nub of clitoris, the swollen cockhead is poised to plunge. . .

Yvette, slinky, dark voyeur lost in the blackness beyond the trelliswork screen, her body deep in the chair in almost a straight line from softly cushioned neck to slowly opening and closing knees, worked two fingers inside her tight, wet little sheath of a cunt as her eyes languidly hovered over the sixty-nine live show but a few feet in front of her while at the same time taking in the ever-changing pornographic display on two adjacent walls above the lovers' heads.

. . . on his knees on the cane sofa, supporting his weight above Belinda's body on a sofa arm, Mikhail has heaved his cock two thirds into her cunt. His hand closest to the camera fiercely grips her ankle, flattening her thigh into her torso all the way up to her neck. Her far leg is bent around his belly so that the penetration is ribaldly back-grounded by its inside thigh, a suspender, and a stocking top. . .

. . . a close-up of Belinda's head and shoulders, a nipple, a knee folded back into frame; her mouth is wide, her eyes are closed – she is ecstatic. . .

As Stan Getz moved into gentle rhythm – 'Round Midnight' – Prince Salamini broke up the sixty-nine. He heaved Frannie on to her knees to face the wall at the head of the bed, got behind her, positioned his glans and slammed his cock all the way up her, making her gasp and close her eyes. Almost as quickly – keen to see the next picture in the porn sequence – she reopened her eyes on Mikhail and Belinda in much the same position as themselves; Belinda on the floor, knees indenting a mauve cushion, cheek flat on a maroon carpet, finger in her mouth as Mikhail, hands tightly clenching her buttocks, gave it to her from behind – except that a more detailed shot revealed that. . .

. . . the young man's cock no longer poles the lady's pussy; it is cramming its dirty way up her back passage and she has a hand between her legs, two middle fingers working their way into her vulva as their companions frame its lips. As Angelo's fucking of Frannie hots up, several more shots of sodomy follow – perhaps the most sala-cious of which has Belinda leaning on her dressing-table, a wonderfully rapturous expres-sion on her face reflected in its mirror above a plate of ripe apples while Mikhail lecherously studies his anal penetration. . .

Yvette floats along with all this stimulation in a

libidinous dream. Like Salamini, an aficionado of Colombian Gold, she has indulged in a plentiful toke before stripping nude to enter the room. As, with a perfect view of his bouncing balls and plunging cock, she gluttonously watches her Italian friend's heaving buttocks and the still, but constantly changing colour shots of enthusiastic buggery above them, she takes herself on a teasing ride towards orgasm. Each time that her climax begins to swoop upon her, her thigh and backside muscles tauten, her pelvis rises from the chair and – by a great effort of will, her teeth baring – she relaxes, fingers motionless inside her. After perhaps a half a minute of drooling at the bed area, she starts her thumb circling gently on her clitoris, her fingers begin yet again to slide within her pussy and the wonderful, groin-invading feelings begin to consume her once more.

Frannie, practised exponent of the multiple orgasm, was certainly not trying to hold back. On the screen in front of her, a second man got into the action. He was as darkly handsome as the first, clad in a loose, square-topped, collarless blue shirt – and nothing else except a hard-on just as impressive as that of his companion. As she studied the huge colour slide a shudder went through her; she squealed, her vagina contracting on Angelo's rutting penis as her climactic juices flowed.

The Italian aristocrat was becoming rather less than princely. His cock rooted deeply within Frannie, he pressed her forward with his hips until she was lying flat on her belly and he on her back. 'You loved the sight of a dick up Belinda's arse, didn't you?' he grunted thickly into her ear, his breath heating it. '*Didn't* you, Frannie?' he insisted, as if defying her to argue.

'No,' she muttered weakly, wriggling her backside against his groin, relishing the feel of his bushy, springy, pubic thatch teasing her buttock flesh.

He chuckled hoarsely. 'Liar!'

As her eyes drifted from the silk of the counterpane beneath her nose to alight once more on a screen – where the action, tri-part now, had shifted to a rose-tinted bed sheet – Angelo withdrew his cock to the glans, paused, then banged it into Frannie hard enough to knock her a couple of inches up the bed and bring a little cry of impassioned hurt to her lips. He pulled it all the way out of her, took his weight on his hands and stroked his cockhead, slippery with her juices, up and down her buttock cleft.

On screen, a most bawdy scene; Belinda is on her side between the two kneeling men, her head cushioned between Blue-Shirt's spread thighs, his thick cock, its base held in his fingers as he stoops over her, sliding into her welcoming mouth. One of her knees is drawn revealingly up to her shoulder. Mikhail kneels across her other thigh, a hand flattened on her buttock, intent on his view of her open pussy as his cock prepares to enter it.

'Shall I bugger you?' Angelo muttered into Frannie's ear, poking his glans at her bottom hole.

'If you like. But be careful,' she whispered, stomach turning itself into a hard knot of excitement, sphincter, perversely, tightening.

At first, as her anus was painfully stretched and she was obliged to squirm forwards and away, panting, 'No. No. *Hold* it,' she thought that it was not going to work – like the most recent attempt in the ruined mill with her husband and Neville Duke. Sodomy being an occasional – but most special – treat, she experienced a pang of regret, her craving having been sharpened by the superb on-screen photos of the lubricious activity. Angelo, however, was prepared.

He rolled off her and reached below the bed to produce a bottle of baby oil, uncapped it and thoroughly lubricated his penis then her tiny hole. He slipped a cushion under her hips to raise her bottom, supported himself on one hand above her, positioned his glans at the entrance to her behind and began to sturdily push.

With Frannie – only vaguely aware that, on screen, Mikhail was poised over Belinda in a press-up attitude with her doubled on her back beneath him, knees splayed around his rigid elbows and sucking Blue-Shirt's cock as Mikhail screwed her – biting her bottom lip and clawing at the precious Indian silk bedspread, Angelo's cock breached the sphincter barrier with relative ease to force its wanton way snugly up her bottom.

The incredibly horny sensation seemed to slide all the way from her bowels, through her chest and into her throat. She squealed. She gasped. She got dirty – 'Oh, yes, do it. *Do* it. Fuck my butt, you *bastard*!' – and, as the cock moved ever faster, deliciously, in her backside, as Angelo's panting became louder, more urgent, as, with the fingers of one hand working furiously beneath her belly she experienced a string of thrilling little orgasms, she kept her eyes glued to the screen in front of them where. . .

. . . Belinda is going through the big one. There can be no doubt about her total absorption in her fucking; with the beaded strap of her slip broken and hanging loose, an ankle perched on Mikhail's now naked shoulder, her head supported on Blue-Shirt's thigh, her hand tensely screwing up the front of his shirt, her eyes tightly closed, her face distorted as if in agony, she silently screams a most powerful climax. . .

Angelo suddenly went still. His buttocks tensed, his thigh muscles bulged. Frannie was mumbling incoherently into the side of her clenched fist. With her fingers stabbing her pussy she jerked her bottom, three times, hard. Wailing 'I'm coming, I'm coming. God, I'm *coming*!' she did just that, plenteously, as the princely seed gushed into her rear end.

All this proved too much for Yvette's controlled wank; she let herself go. Her body arched off the chair until it was supported only between her rigid toes and her shoulders with three fingers jammed up her pussy to their bases she loudly yelped – then yelped again.

Salamini rolled off Frannie on to his back, glistening cock in rapid decline, his hand outflung over her buttocks and his chest rising and falling as if he had just completed a marathon.

Frannie remained prostrate, a hand lodged between her thighs, heart thumping, eyes closed, wallowing in the twin sensations of the wetness of her pussy and the throbbing of her bottom.

After a while, as Getz did amazing things with 'East of the Sun', Frannie opened her eyes on the screen in front of them where a new series of pictures featuring a muscular negro and a frail and lovely blonde masseuse was evolving. Without looking away from a raunchy slide of the girl fishing a truly massive erection from the negro's pants, Frannie remarked, 'Great sound effects you have here, Angelo.' She raised her voice. 'So why don't you come here and *join* us, Yvette?'

6

WOLFGANG BANG

EARLY EVENING NAPS REVIVED THEM from the effects of the excesses of a lengthy afternoon's indulgence in heavy sex; during a splendid fondue meal in the hotel's candlelit restaurant both Frannie and Prince Salamini appeared remarkably fresh. As her final little chunk of the tenderest venison simmered on its skewer in boiling oil, Frannie noticed that the hunky, blond gentleman she had been so taken with during brunch was tucked away – once again on his own – eating in a far corner of the room. She pointed him out to Salamini, curious to discover if the prince knew who he was.

He glanced over his shoulder at the man, then raised an eyebrow at Frannie. 'You perhaps have ambitions in that direction?' he asked her.

She smiled as she drew her cooked meat out of the oil and waved it in the air to cool. 'There *is* something about him,' she confessed. 'He's most attractive.' She popped the venison in her mouth.

'And you'll no doubt be delighted to know he's as colourful as his appearance suggests. He is Austrian, his name is Wolfgang von Schwerin. He is very rich – he owns a small private bank whose name for the moment escapes me.' He paused, studying Frannie enigmatically. 'And he has a certain reputation as far as the fair sex is concerned.'

'Ah.'

'Also, there is recent infamy attached to him. A gruesome murder. Somewhat of a mystery. Would you like to hear about it?'

He told her how the man's young wife had been found dead on her bed the previous year, most bloodily murdered. Von Schwerin had a palatial home near Lucerne on the Lake of the Cantons. There had been rumours of a man living wild in the mountains behind his house, signs of forced entry. His wife had been sexually assaulted, tied and carved up with a knife. She had bled to death, the wild man had never been hunted down. The case remained open. . .

'I'll introduce you, if you wish,' Angelo offered.

Wolfgang von Schwerin joined them for coffee. At close quarters, Frannie found his eyes quite amazing; every time he looked at her they seemed to reach out and grab hers in a thrillingly icy grip. It was almost mesmerising. He had a quiet way of talking with his clipped Austrian accent which compelled one to listen. When Frannie explained to him that she had broken a trip on the Orient Express to stop off in Zurich he said, 'The next one through is, I believe, on Monday? You will then be rejoining this train?'

'Yes. I arranged to meet my friends in Venice to start back on Wednesday. They're going to wait there for me, so leaving here on Monday will be perfect. It gives me tomorrow here.' She smiled meaningfully at her prince, flickering her eyelids.

'I rather *like* it here.'

To Frannie's slight touch of regret, the Austrian shortly left them. The rest of the evening – and much of the night – passed in enjoyable, often amazing, sexual contortions with Angelo and Yvette, both of whom appeared to be insatiable. At one stage in the dissolute proceedings Angelo and Frannie tied the black girl to the inside of the silver lattice bed screen, spreadeagled and once again gagged with Frannie's knickers. They tortured her by leaving her trussed and without carnal contact of any sort for an hour while they riotously fucked to a background of continuously projected porn slides. Freed at last, she had behaved like some sex-crazed wildcat, trying to ravish them both at the same time as her body was wracked with a whole string of orgasms.

Yet despite her repletion, the following day whilst enjoying a pre-lunch aperitif with Matilda, Frannie found herself musing about the hypnotic von Schwerin and wondering what it might be like to make love with him. As if her thought waves had somehow reached him, suddenly there he was with his shiny blond ponytail, wearing an immaculate, midnight-blue suit. He politely asked if he might join them and invite them for a drink.

'I have been having some thoughts about your trip,' he told Frannie, as freshly charged glasses arrived. 'I believe I could perhaps make it that much more interesting for you?'

'How do you propose to do that?' she asked him. She experienced a faint, familiar flutter of excitement as she realised that a proposition was imminent – a proposition, moreover, that she was likely to accept since there was no doubt in her libido that she very much wanted to sport with this gorgeous specimen of manhood in his bed – or wherever he preferred to do such things.

'I am returning to my house this afternoon. I have a helicopter waiting to transport me. You would be most welcome to join me.'

Frannie carefully sipped her martini, watching him over the rim of the glass; those extraordinary eyes captured hers as they had done the evening before, and refused to let go. They induced a tingling thrill in her spine, making the tiny hairs of its skin prickle. Slowly, she said, 'Of course I would have to sort it out with Prince Salamini. I am his guest, after all.'

'Naturally.'

'And I would want that Matilda, and my man Gregory, accompany me. I never travel without them.'

'I have a large helicopter. And an even larger house.'

Angelo Salamini was perfectly charming about it. He in any case had important business, he told her, early the following morning for which he needed to be fresh and alert. Then he was off to New York.

So the brief Salamini episode was over. Well and good. It had been vastly entertaining and enormously sexually satisfying, but enough, for her ladyship, was enough – especially when new adventure beckoned. She had a lengthy record of the AC/DC dalliance on video for the mutual enjoyment of her and her husband on her return, and some great scenes to describe if ever she should decide to pen another novel. On with the new!

One and a half hours later, with Wolfgang von Schwerin himself piloting his helicopter, Frannie and party were being lifted above the city of Zurich from where they headed off south-west towards the centre of Switzerland.

It was the perfect way, on what was a balmy summer's day, to be travelling through that enchanting country. They cut down amongst comparatively low mountains where the snows had melted to expose lush, emerald-green meadows dotted with neat, perfectly kept houses and cabins, most of them timbered and with angular roofs and shutters of bright red, blue, or green, all of these dwellings at different levels and each in its individual way delightful; the overall impression was of flying above a sort of affluent fairyland.

It was a short hop of forty kilometres, only fifteen minutes. The spectacular, snow-capped mountains of the south drew ever closer and sunlight bounced dazzlingly up at the chopper as they sped over the lake on which sits the charming town of Zug. As they approached the Lake of the Cantons the gloriously pretty Lucerne with its sprinkling of elegant turrets became clear as a picture postcard; entranced with it all, Matilda even managed to overcome her terror of being airborne.

Wolfgang's house was perched right on the edge of the lake. It was grandly beautiful after the wedding-cake fashion of many Swiss houses,

113

white walled and on three levels, and occasionally four. It was crowned with three castle-like turrets and two roofs constructed in an assortment of eye-catching angles. The windows – and there were more than fifty of them – were flanked with scarlet-painted wooden shutters in startling contrast to the walls. The house – which was as large as an hotel – was back-dropped by a pine-wooded mountain; rearing directly up behind it and barely leaving room for a garden it soared beyond the wood to rich, steep, house-dotted meadows and finally into a craggy, snow-covered peak.

The helicopter pad was in the small garden. Settling down on it was vaguely scary, the necessity of almost tucking into the mountain producing an illusion of danger. Matilda failed to get the jitters only because she had removed her spectacles in order to avoid having to witness the landing.

There was another, unnerving aspect about arriving at the unimaginatively named Villa du Lac; the manservant. As soon as the helicopter rotor blades ceased their windy motion he lumbered up heavily to open a door. Dressed in a spotless, white monkey jacket and flawlessly creased black and white pinstriped trousers whose turn-ups fell perfectly on gleaming black, size seventeen shoes, he was a flat-faced, bald-headed giant with hands as big as boxing gloves. Gregory, always averse to being upstaged in the beef department, gave the man a sideways look which might have been construed as being hostile as he stepped down from the helicopter.

Von Schwerin addressed the servant – who was inches larger than Gregory all over – as Adolf.

'I don't know that I'm entirely happy, luvvy,' commented Matilda shortly afterwards while, in a sun-filled room with a splendid view over the lake, she began to unpack Frannie's case.

'Why not?' asked Frannie. She was changing into a fresh, plain white cotton blouse. 'It's beautiful here.'

'I dunno. I feel a mite uneasy. Our host is beautiful, too, but something about him gives me the willies. Those eyes! And as for that manservant. Ugh. Besides which, we were supposed to be taking a trip on the Orient Express.'

'We are. We'll be back on it in a couple of days or so.' The blouse was tightly stretched over Frannie's full breasts, her nipples saucily jutting. She left the top three buttons undone to expose deep, eye-catching cleavage, and turned up the collar.

'Seduction, is it?' asked Matilda. She paused in the act of hanging up a dress to gaze with her usual admiration at her mistress.

'Whatever makes you think that?'

'I'd have a care if I were you. I really would.'

'Stop fussing, Matilda. The man owns a bank, for Heaven's sake.'

Matilda sniffed. 'I'm not sure if *that's* in his favour!'

'And as it happens I find friend Adolf a comforting presence.' As she touched up her make-up, Frannie related Prince Salamini's story about the murder.

Aghast, Matilda said, 'You mean there's some wild lunatic up there in the mountain just waiting his opportunity to slink in here and cut our throats?' She shivered.

'I doubt if he's around any more.'

'But the police never caught him?'

'No. They . . . ' she was interrupted by the internal phone ringing. It was Wolfgang, suggesting that he and Frannie took a late afternoon trip on the lake and she happily agreed.

His boat was a sleek, modern, fifty-foot cabin cruiser. As, with Adolf at the helm, they slid out of the boathouse, one of the immaculate passenger steamers which was styled after a Mississippi riverboat and had a regular schedule around a number of small towns bordering the lake, chugged by; they were rocked pleasantly by its wake.

The air was crisp and clean, the dipping sun warm enough for Frannie to feel through her blouse as she sat, legs crossed, short cream skirt riding high on her bare thighs, sipping a vodka tonic. She and the Austrian were comfortably settled on deck in heavy cane chairs amongst cushions embroidered with Indian dancing girls. The panorama through which they cut their steady path was supremely lovely, utterly relaxing. Houses, hotels, small towns were pristine, all seemingly freshly painted; behind them the land, so green you could smell it, reared up into the snowline and startlingly white, rugged peaks.

Von Schwerin – and Frannie was gratified by it – was not one of those men who find it necessary to impress a woman with a constant stream of witty stories. He chatted only intermittently, leaving her free to enjoy the view, occasionally pointing out landmarks and places of interest.

When they had been on the lake for over half an hour and were passing a passenger stage with no town behind it he pointed up a very steep, woody slope to where on a high pole, alone in the middle of a field, the Swiss flag limply fluttered.

'That is where Switzerland first became one country,' he told her. 'Five hundred years ago the leaders of the cantons met there and agreed to join forces.'

Frannie was surprised. 'Way up there, in an isolated field. Why?'

'They were rebels, opponents of outside rule. The meeting was secret, the venue central to most cantons and – as you can see – virtually unassailable.' Unexpectedly – he had made no sexual move towards her so far except with his eyes – he leant forward to put a hand on her bare knee. His piercing look punched its way through her blouse. The hand squeezed and slipped an inch or so upwards. 'Open air union,' he said. 'Does the idea perhaps agree with you?'

She found staring levelly back at him without betraying the effect those eyes and the hand were having on her almost impossible. 'I can't imagine what you mean,' she weakly lied.

'Making love in the open air?'

'I understood we were discussing Swiss history?'

'We were. We are now talking about sex.' The marauding hand slid a little higher.

'*You* are,' she pointed out.

She closed her hand over his and pushed it back to her knee; not that she did not find its encroachment powerfully welcome, but she felt she perhaps ought to make some gesture of resistance, however feeble.

'Why did you so readily accept my invitation here?'

'Curiosity. I happen to have a highly developed sense of adventure.'

'And that would embrace sex?'

'Perhaps.'

'And do you enjoy making love in the open?' His hand, hers resting lightly upon it, insisted its way up her thigh until its thumb was touching the hem of her skirt.

Nervously swallowing her drink, eager to be in his arms, she managed without stammering to say, 'That would depend upon with whom.'

'You happen to be with me.' His thumb explored beneath her skirt hem, digging into the softness of her inner thigh.

Frannie glanced over her shoulder at the wheelhouse. 'And there *happens* to be someone watching us.'

'This is easy to remedy. We shall drop anchor and I will send him below.' He stood, leaning over her, his free hand finding her other thigh, both of them flatly sliding under her skirt until the tips of his index fingers lightly touched the crotch of her knickers. His lips, warm and confident, brushed hers. 'Okay?'

'Okay,' she whispered, belly tense with excitement.

Minutes later, they were at the banks of the lake, nosed partially beneath a weeping willow tree, and Adolf was dropping anchor; that done, he disappeared below.

'He never says a word,' Frannie observed.

'He's dumb. I like it that way.'

Taking her in his arms, Wolfgang again brushed his lips against hers; but he seemed to entertain minimal interest in kissing her mouth. As he pressed her into him, his lips travelled slowly over her cheek to her neck until he was nibbling the edge of her earlobe next to where the fastener for her large, gold, hoop earrings passed through it. She wriggled more tightly into him, delighted to feel a solid hard-on digging into her lower belly through his cotton trousers. Another cock, attached to yet another handsome man, was about to be hers; she felt, as she invariably did during such moments with a new lover-to-be, weak, vulnerable and almost unbearably excited, shamelessly craving the pleasures of an untried prick.

The Austrian spent minimal time on preliminaries; he rucked up Frannie's little skirt until it was sitting on her hips, he thumbed her knickers down almost to her knees and, with his hands invading her buttocks, he crouched in front of her, inspected her naked pussy with eyes in which had suddenly appeared the weird light of an almost crazy carnality then plunged his nose into her bush and his tongue into her vulva.

Taken by surprise by the unexpectedly rapid assault upon her person, by this unbelievably swift baring and eating of her pussy, inflamed by

119

it, gasping, Frannie sagged at the knees and clawed at the bobbing, ponytailed head, widening her thighs as far as the drooping panties would allow and shoving her crotch hungrily against the man's face.

Von Schwerin turned practically savage. His tongue was out of Frannie's pussy as quickly as it had dived its way in. Ice-eyes discordant like those of a drunk, he heaved himself to his feet, tossed cushions from the chairs to the deck and grappled her to her knees with her elbows propped on a chair. As she peered – her slight alarm overwhelmed by her lust – over her shoulder, he ripped open his belt and his zipper, dragged trousers and pants down to expose a hefty, throbbing, swaying erection, dropped to his feet at her bottom, clumsily found her cunt lips with his glans and shoved his cock all the way up her with such force that the chair scraped on the deck as his hips banged into her buttocks and his balls slapped between the backs of her thighs.

Frannie is riding too high a sexual wave to be bothered by the modicum of pain which this animal penetration brings her. As von Schwerin fucks her from behind with all the power of a rutting bull she grunts and mewls her pleasure into the corner of a cushion which is soon sopping with her saliva; this is perhaps the most rapid first-time breaching of her life and her belly is filled with such fire that it threatens to consume her as the Austrian cock rams in and out of her and the satisfyingly heavy balls knock into the back of her thighs.

It is undoubtedly just as well that Frannie has her back to the man and therefore cannot see the expression on his face; all the attractiveness has been wiped off; it is a livid, snarling mask of lust; more, it has turned horribly cruel. As von Schwerin ruts away with his trousers shuddering around his knees, his expression is one of utter loathing. He mutters unintelligibly to himself, he dribbles, his eyes roll around in his head.

His hands steal beneath her breasts, he rips apart the buttons of her blouse, tearing one off in the process, he squeezes her tits hurtfully together and then, as his fucking speeds up, his cock pistoning, he holds her tits in fists which cling to them as if they are his solitary lifeline to the world.

He comes, this mad beast. Scarcely three minutes after entering Frannie he climaxes with a bellow which echoes off the historical mountain-side above the boat. His seed erupts in great gushes within Frannie's pussy; the sudden flooding, the familiar, welcome, sticky heat, together contrive to bring her off with a shout of her own.

He comes – and he comes – orgasm ripping through his body in gigantic spasms and as he does so he grunts in German – a language merci-fully not understood by her ladyship – 'I'm going to kill you, you fucking bitch. I'm going to kill you, Alexandra!'

Von Schwerin's body flops over Frannie's back as the last of his semen spurts into her. 'Kill you,' he mutters again, into her ear. He is still, except for his chest which rises and falls agitatedly against her back.

'Jesus. Oh, Jesus, was that ever fucking good!'

Frannie mumbles into the Indian lady embroidered on the cushion.

Lengthy moments passed before Wolfgang heaved his heavy weight from Frannie. His limp penis flopped out of her, trailing damply over a buttock. He swayingly stood. She clambered awkwardly up off her cramped and dented knees. Quite oblivious to the fact that, less than a hundred yards away, a passenger boat was slowly sliding by, they each tiredly pulled up their pants as several people looked astoundedly on.

'Because it is my first time with you, this was quick,' muttered Wolfgang. The madness had vanished from his face to be replaced by a slack-jowled languor. 'This is often so. But this night I have a part of my house to take you into where we shall considerably extend our physical knowledge of one another. I believe it is going to greatly surprise you.'

As night began to fall a chill crept into the air. Whilst fifteen minutes or so distant from Villa du Lac, they went below. There, in a luxuriously appointed cabin with teak bulkheads and an abundance of highly polished brass fittings, Frannie picked up a silver framed photograph of a beautiful young lady to examine it with wide eyes. 'I could have sworn for a minute that you had somehow got hold of a picture of me,' she told von Schwerin. 'She must be my double.'

He looked at her oddly. 'There is a remarkable resemblance, is there not?' he agreed. 'She is – was – my wife. Sadly, she was murdered last year. Poor Alexandra.'

7

HORROGRAM

SO, THERE WAS I, POOR innocent that I am, unknowingly headed for trouble yet again! Ahah – you may well remark – how is it that Francesca Jones can write about the man's cruelly contorted features when she states 'Frannie has her back to the man and therefore cannot see the expression on his face'?

The answer is that you must grant me a certain amount of poetic licence. I was to witness that frightening face – as you will read – at close quarters later on, and have with hindsight assumed, remembering his guttural German whilst he was bonking me – in which I have also indulged myself in the translation – that that was more or less how it must have been during those moments. You must remember that whilst all my stories are in essence factual, they are a novelisation of what happens to me in which I allow myself artistic freedom.

I suppose I should have suspected a degree of madness to be lurking in the depths of such unbelievably hypnotic eyes and that I might be in the clutches of a dangerous psychopath; Matilda was certainly more than a mite uneasy in that house, I ought to have paid heed to her. But you know what I'm like with a new man, how I tend to get carried away, blinded by sex.

That evening, during a splendid candlelit dinner for two in a dining room overlooking the moonwashed lake, von Schwerin – who could not have been a more charming host – informed me that he had a most special room in the house, a room the like of which almost certainly existed nowhere else in the universe.

A room especially designed for sex, naturally.

Gosh – I thought – do all macho males with property in Switzerland have their homes equipped with sex rooms? But I did not voice this question. And he was not exaggerating. When I was introduced to the place I found myself staggered; by comparison Prince Salamini's playroom was almost as tame as a children's nursery!

* * *

On a smallish landing at the top of a four-storey tower, Wolfgang von Schwerin, with Frannie, paused in front of an ornamental oak door to open, with a key, a panel set in the wall at its side; he pressed some mysterious buttons within. Lifting a cautionary finger to his lips he said, 'We must slip inside very quietly. I have some friends in there. They will not object to our presence, but we should disturb them as little as possible. You will appreciate why in a moment.'

Friends? – Frannie had been aware of no one in the house except for themselves, Matilda and Gregory, and the servants.

He silently opened the door and took Frannie inside into almost darkness, shutting them in. She suppressed a gasp; maybe ten feet away from them on a bed arrangement at floor level, were three people.

A scintillatingly gorgeous young lady with waist-length blonde hair was lounging against big, soft cushions between two muscular negroes who were clad only in white, cut-off jeans. The solitary source of light seemed to be an invisible one which illuminated them. The girl was dressed in underwear – a lacy white bra, a matching slip, black stockings. As Frannie, in mild shock, scarcely daring to breath, watched, the blonde glanced towards the newcomers, but only for a moment and with no greeting in her expression. Then she looked hard at the bulging crotch of one of the negroes – neither of whom had acknowledged the intruders in any way – and said, softly and distinctly, her green-nailed hand reaching for his zipper, 'Okay, you guys, I guess it's about time we fucked.'

The sound of the zipper being slicked down appeared unnaturally loud. The girl pulled the man's shorts to his thighs – he was naked beneath them – and stooped over him to take his limp, fat penis into her mouth.

It was extraordinary to have walked in unannounced on such salacious activity and even more so that the trio were acting as if Frannie and von Schwerin were not there.

'Come.' The Austrian took Frannie by the hand to lead her around to one side of the floor-bed, to sit on a wide, low level sofa. By the time they had settled down, the black cock was growing between the blonde's lips and the other man – in no need of such help to get it up – had removed his shorts to reveal a huge erection. He pulled the girl's slip up above suspenderless stocking tops; beneath she was knickerless, her pussy hair so blonde it might have been dyed.

Briefly unmouthing her cock she mumbled, whilst fisting it hard, 'Gonna stick it in me, Joe? Gonna stick your big dong right up my cooze?'

'You bet your sweet life, honey,' said Joe in a southern accent. He completed the task of piling her slip on to her waist, angled her sideways and opened her pussy. 'Gonna feed you a real solid fuck.'

'It's what she needs, the cock-sucker,' muttered the other man as she returned to doing just that. 'Ain't it, Suzy, you fuckin' cock-sucker?' She moaned into her mouthful of ebony penis as Joe's eight or so thick inches slid deeply inside her from behind.

Frannie was fighting with herself to come to terms with what was going on here; there was, of course, no doubt that this heavy scene had been masterfully set up by her host, but nevertheless it took some getting accustomed to. Despite that, she felt herself dampening between her legs as Joe heaved his cock in and out of Suzy's blonde-fuzzed cunt while she gave ever more enthusiastic head to the as yet anonymous other negro.

'An arousing performance, is it not?' murmured Wolfgang.

'I'll say,' she whispered. She had changed for

dinner into a mauve, ankle-length, lightweight Balenciaga evening dress embroidered with silver sequins. Without warning, his hand suddenly shot all the way under its skirt to her Christian Dior silk-cosseted crotch.

'So, already you are wet,' he breathed into her ear. She wriggled as a finger found its way beneath her knickers and inside her.

'You bet I'm wet. God!'

'Get down on me? Get it out and go down on me.'

With a second finger slipping inside her pussy and the two black studs changing position, Suzy getting on her knees between them, Frannie unzipped Wolfgang and fished out his hard-on, ducking her head to it with her eyes swivelled to the three-way fuck action as Joe's friend's name was revealed.

'Shove it all the way in to your bollocks, Andy,' Suzy insisted. As he obliged with a massive jerk of taut, glistening buttocks, thigh muscles bulging, she gobbled fiercely on kneeling Joe's cock.

The room was filled with the steamy sounds of heavy sex; Andy's thigh tops loudly slapping into Suzy's backside – her bottom's snowy whiteness a delicious contrast to his black skin; both men grunting; her mouth slurping on Joe's cock; Wolfgang's heavy panting as Frannie sucked him and massaged his balls.

Without warning, as speedily as he had done on the boat, von Schwerin climaxed. His hips arched off the sofa, his fingers stilled in Frannie's pussy, he shouted something in German and his seed spilled into Frannie's mouth. Enjoying the taste, unsatisfied herself, Frannie swallowed the sperm, unmouthed the deflating cock and ran a tongue-tip all around her lips. As the Austrian hand fell limply away from her pussy she replaced it with her own, fingers jabbing, eyes feasting on the triple swing.

Von Schwerin made a quick recovery. Taking hold of his wilted cock which protruded, with his balls, through still belted, dark silk trousers, he mumbled, 'Perhaps you would like to join my friends?'

Close to orgasm, trembling with lust, Frannie took up the challenge with unseemly haste; she stood, yanked her dress over her head and tossed it away from her, climbed rapidly out of her knickers and – as the rutting threesome rolled on to their sides, Andy's cock buried in Suzy's cunt – she eagerly got down on the bed and reached for Joe's cock which was once more seeking the blonde's lips.

Frannie grabbed erect black penis – and her hand went right through it! For the moment assuming there must be something odd about the lighting, she tried again; her hand passed through the man's genitals and on through his groin as his prick found its way deep into Suzy's mouth.

Flabbergasted, Frannie waved her hand about as if feeling for something in the dark; there was nothing, merely empty space inhabited by energetically coupling, perfectly solid-looking people. Hearing von Schwerin's lazy laughter, she looked at him in astonishment. 'What the bloody hell *is* this?' she asked him.

'A hologram,' he told her. 'The most advanced in the world.' Reaching behind him, he flicked a switch; the rutting threesome vanished, low lighting illuminated a seemingly impossible empty bed.

'I don't believe it,' said Frannie. 'They were *real*, for Christ's sake. They were speaking and breathing.'

'And fucking. You are privileged to have been watching the world's first technologically perfect pornographic hologram. I have a great deal of money invested in its business future.' As he spoke he was playing with himself, a strange light in his eyes, penis on the rise again as if the very fact of explaining to her about the hologram was sexual stimulation in itself.

Frannie continued to gaze at the empty bed incredulously as she came, with difficulty, to terms with the idea that what they had been viewing were only laser-produced images. After a while she glanced around the room, her eyes seeking the source; there was little to see beyond four unobtrusive speakers and some small holes in the maroon flock wallpaper – evidently they were false and the projection equipment was behind them. Apart from the sofa, and its twin, and the almost floor-level bed, there was no furniture.

For the first time she noticed that the Austrian was determinedly masturbating – and getting it up again. It occurred to her that she had not climaxed and she realised that Wolfgang was wanking at the sight of her – knickerless and wearing only a frivolous little suspender belt, sheer, light purple stockings and black spiky-heeled patent leather evening shoes. She assumed that the weird light which burned in his narrowed eyes – and might have been a sign of madness – was merely a manifestation of gluttonous desire. She pressed the ball of her thumb into her pubis as she rolled her thighs together. 'Is there more film?' she hopefully asked.

'*She* used to like to watch me wank,' was his irrelevant reply, his cock getting good and hard as he said it.

'Did she?' Frannie steered away from the presumably delicate subject of the man's murdered wife. Clutching her pussy, index finger probing, raunchiness returning with a vengeance, she muttered, 'Maybe you'd like to watch *me*?'

'You and my friends at the same time.'

He flicked switches, the lights went out. As if by miracle, Suzy and her black studs materialised in precisely the same positions from which they had vanished, the blonde avidly sucking Joe's cock while Andy strenuously fucked her from behind.

'Sit there,' said Wolfgang as he placed a cushion on the arm of a sofa. He had her straddle the cushion, facing him, pussy gaudily exposed in the dimly reflected light from the copulating images.

For a while, as they hornily watched the impossibly real illusion and listened to a continuous stream of obscenities from non-existent lips, Lady Ballington and Wolfgang von Schwerin committed the onanistic sin together.

So engrossed in the contortions of the trio did Frannie become that she had almost forgotten the presence of her wanking companion until he grunted – as Suzy changed position to squat on supine Joe, facing him, while Andy moved in on his knees behind her – 'Fuck me, Frannie. Get on it.'

Frannie's attention strays from the hologram as she sits next to Wolfgang, unbelts his trousers and yanks them, together with yellow slips, to his knees. She half stands, cocks a leg over his and with her back to him fishes beneath her bottom for his cock. With Andy's voice dragging her eyes back to the bed as he says, 'Gonna cram my dick all the way up there with Joe's. Here comes the stuffing of your life, honey,' Frannie sinks down to fully impale herself on the teutonic cock. It disappears inside her, its welcome heat deep within her belly, his balls jammed against her pussy lips.

Suzy wails – 'Aaaaiiiiii!' – as Andy crouches over her back, legs apart to offer a graphic view as he carries out his promise. With Wolfgang jerking his bottom beneath her Frannie bounces on his prick. Both their gazes are most lecherously hooked on the bed where Andy squashes his big tool up Suzy's cunt back to back with Joe's, all the way in until his balls crush into those of his friend.

'Jesus fuck, you filthy bastards, Jesus fuck, Jesus *fuck*,' goes Suzy, her head ecstatically rolling to trail her hair over the bed. With her weight on one arm she stretches a hand between her legs to toy with the two jiggling scrotums. 'How does it feel . . .' she hoarsely mutters, 'your two black meat slabs rubbing against one another? You like it? You *like* that, mother-fuckers?'

'We ain't gay, lady,' protests Andy. As if to emphasise the point he slides his cock nearly out of her and slams it back in, almost throwing her forward on to her face when his testicles bang against Joe's.

'Maybe, but you *love* it, don't you?' she pants. 'You like your filthy dicks all buddy-buddy in my cooze. Don't you? Don't you, *fuckers*?'

'Yeah,' says Joe, heaving his bottom off the bed. 'You're right – we love it. But not as much as you, you fucking nympho. Gonna fuck you half to death.'

All this obscene debauchery is a little too much for Frannie who in her fertile imagination can smell their sweat and feel the heat of their breath. She jumps her pussy up and down on Wolfgang's cock, tip of her index finger going wild on her clitoris, tits bouncing, hair flying, comes with a little shout, comes again – and keeps on furiously riding a prick which she knows is about to prematurely erupt again because its owner is groaning words of German and panting and gasping.

She cannot see the crazy, hate-filled expression which contorts his features.

An invisible magician waves his phallic wand; a third naked man appears on the bed. He is white, early middle-aged, balding and somewhat over-weight. But his cock, flaccid, dangles a third of the way down his almost hairless thigh and his balls are as large as tangerines. He leeringly drops to his knees in front of Suzy. 'Head,' he growls.

Suzy scoops up the outsized glans of this circumsised cock with the end of her tongue and laps it into her mouth as the negroes continue to pound her overstuffed pussy. It grows, that lily-white prick, with astonishing speed as Suzy licks and gobbles it. In less than a minute, much larger than either of the black cocks, it is all the way up and the blonde is able to accommodate little more than its great head between her stretched lips.

'Me and the boys are going to give you a come-bath, Sue. Going to soak you in real hot and juicy spunk,' mutters the white man as Suzy fists his balls and he jerks his hips.

The screwing – except for Frannie's – comes to an end. Frannie is riding a massive high; hands flat on Wolfgang's knees above his half-mast pants and gaping trouser top, eyes positively dopy with sex, she is sliding up and down his greasy pole of a prick from its tip to his balls, impaling herself with orgiastic determination as she watches Suzy get on her back.

Joe, slack mouthed, goes on his knees between Suzy's spread legs, jerking himself off as Andy does the same thing over her belly and the white man kneels by her face and fucks her mouth.

Muttering to himself in German, grasping Frannie's tits with the same, sadistic force as he had on the boat, Wolfgang comes inside her. Almost there for perhaps the dozenth time herself, as she feels the surge of wetness in her pussy, Frannie sits all the way down on his erupting cock and stills, tip of her finger trembling on her clitoris as she tries to time her climax to coincide with what is about to happen on the bed.

It is indeed a come-bath. As the men shoot over Suzy the impression is that they must have been saving it up for days; Andy is first, directing his seed over her belly and her tits; Joe and the white man come almost together, Joe soaking her thighs and her pussy, then mingling his sperm with Andy's puddle on her belly as the cock in Suzy's mouth starts to fill it, is withdrawn, and erupts over her lips, her cheeks and her throat.

Whilst this grossly ribald act is taking place, Frannie is utterly consumed with an orgasm which has her shuddering and shaking, her vagina going through a string of contractions on the cock which, embedded in it, is already beginning to shrink. Her climax rips on until after the final drop of sperm besmirches Suzy's quiveringly acquiescent flesh. As the naked figures suddenly fade away, Frannie collapses silently sideways off Wolfgang's lap and on to the sofa.

Quick to come – in Frannie's book firmly down as a 'wham, bang, thank you ma'am' merchant – Wolfgang is even quicker to recover. Seconds later, as he pulled up his trousers and pants, he said, 'I am willing to bet, Frannie, that you get a thrill from the playing of games.'

She opened one eye in time to observe his cock and balls flop upwards before disappearing beneath his yellow underpants. 'Depends,' she said, with a yawn, rolling on to her back, sitting up and running a lazy hand through her disarranged hair. 'And, by the way, at the moment I'm just the tiniest bit spent.'

He jerked up his zipper. Fastening his belt buckle he told her, 'You have all the time you wish to recover.'

'Good of you,' she said drily, with a twisted little smile.

'How would a bondage-rape game meet with your approval?'

Unstartled – the man was a number one weirdo, after all – she nodded towards the bed. 'Is there no more of that? It was, my *God* it was....'

'Was it not? Sadly, no, that was my first set.' His eyes roved over her in odd little jerks as he ran the back of his knuckles from one of her nipples to the other and down to her belly where he nestled them in her bush. 'We can see it again some other time. Meanwhile, why do you not slip your dress on and we'll go to the comfort of your bedroom?'

She experienced the faintest tremor of doubt. Those eyes again; so strange, so compelling in their icy blueness, yet somehow out of synchronisation as they wandered over her nakedness and down to his muff-nuzzling knuckles. 'All right,' she agreed, '. . . but nothing rough, okay? I'm not into serious S & M. As long as it *is* no more than games playing you want, then fine.'

'Yes, but of course, my dear. And with what I propose that we do together, you will discover I maintain my erection even longer.'

Even *longer*? mused her ladyship. The expression was pure arrogance in view of his unimpressive performance so far – not that she was not having a libidinously marvellous time. She reached for her knickers. 'All right. Let's go.'

He stopped her hand. 'You will not be needing those. Just your dress in case we should bump into a servant on the way.'

'Are you recovered?' he asked her, in her bedroom.

'I guess,' she told him, curiosity – and juices – stirring as she stood looking at the bed with its shiny, ornamental brass head and foot.

'Then this is what I should like you to do. Disrobe and . . .', he produced a diaphanous, pale blue nightdress from a wardrobe, bunched it and tossed it to her, '. . . put on this.' Going to the French windows he opened one door fractionally; there was a balcony behind it. 'Leave this ajar and when I leave lock the door behind me. Get ready, turn the lights out and go to bed. I shall play the part of the marauder, sneaking in through your balcony window, tying you up.' He paused, eyes slitting. 'Raping you.'

'I'm not so sure if . . .'

'Come *on*. You must be able to trust me by now?'

'Yes, but . . .' once again she failed to finish her sentence as she was hooked by those shifting, shining eyes, wondering if, ultimately, she *should* trust this very peculiar man. Again, she recalled Matilda's reservations.

'Naturally, I shall expect you to resist. But not so very much, you understand. It is only an adult game.'

'Good, clean fun for the kiddies?' she muttered.

He flashed remarkably even, very white teeth. 'Something like that. You are going to love it, that I promise you.'

'Well – all right.'

'I'll give you five minutes.'

He left, and she locked the door. Going to the open window, she glanced outside; the balcony went past the window of the room next door. Of course, he planned to make his entrance from there. She realised that she had the option of locking the window and backing out of this; but that would hardly be the adventure-seeking Frannie Ballington. Besides, she was beginning to get excited at the prospect of what lay ahead, and the slight trepidation she was experiencing merely added to that excitement; she realised she was feeling a bit like she had done that time not so long ago in Hollywood when superstar Chester Becker had insisted they make love in a patio with his two pet gorillas wandering free around them.*

Her eye fell on the video bag which she had neglected to take to the sex room. Well – she decided – *this* scene would not go unrecorded. She set it up on the bedside table so that the hidden, wide-angle lens had perfect coverage of the bed, swiftly got undressed – leaving her clothes strewn over the floor – climbed into bed and turned off the lights. After a minute or so she set the infra-red film silently rolling.

Through the window, the night sky was bright with stars. Frannie could not see the moon, but its

_____

* *Frannie Goes to Hollywood*

light, and its reflected light from the lake, infused the room with a pale and – under the circumstances – eerie glow. Pulling the sheet and blanket up to her neck, scarlet-nailed fingers tensely gripping the greeny, turned-over top of the sheet, she waited, eyes on the window, aware of the thumping of her heart.

It was rather like a Count Dracula movie; a dark shadow suddenly blocked out most of the light from the window as Wolfgang von Schwerin, clad in an ankle-length, black towelling dressing gown, appeared and stepped through it. He paused on the threshold, chuckling, sounding most evil.

'It is useless to scream,' he said. 'I know that you are quite alone in the house.'

It was only an act, but Frannie, the consummate actress when it was called for, managed to induce within herself a soupçon of fear. 'You – you stay away from me,' she muttered.

Swift as a pouncing tiger, he was on her. Her gasp was loud and for real as he dragged the bedclothes off of her, leapt on to the bed, forced his knees between her legs and tore the front of her nightdress completely open.

She made the obligatory fake attempt to roll off the bed. He swooped down upon her to pin her to the mattress with his weight on a forearm across the top of her breasts. As she struggled and protested beneath him he slipped the sash of his dressing gown from its loops; with its ends he tied her wrists to the brass bedhead struts, her hands stretched two feet or so apart above her head. Mouthing feeble protest she twisted and turned her body beneath him but – already getting well into the sexual swing of things – she did not make his task of dominating her too difficult.

With a satisfied sigh he dropped back on his haunches and as he did so the front of his dressing gown fell open, revealing to his 'victim' the welcome fact that he was sporting a throbbing hard-on.

But the bondage was not yet complete; he used her nightdress belt to tie one of her ankles to a post at the foot of the bed, then he took the hem of the nightdress and savagely tore a strip from it which he used to secure her other ankle to the opposite post. Climbing off the bed he shrugged out of his gown and stood, clutching the brass rails between Frannie's bare, trapped, scarlet-tipped feet, leering at her naked body with its ripped, wide-flung nightdress clinging still to her arms.

Aware what a salacious sight she presented thus spread-eagled and helpless, Frannie fixed her eyes on, between the brass bars at the foot of the bed, the pony-tailed naked Austrian's prick swaying, as, lips trembling in lust, he growled at her, 'You may as well settle back and enjoy this, lovely lady.'

He walked around the bed, cock in hand, and clambered on to it to straddle her tits, stroking himself, his testicles wobbling close to her chin – exactly the close-up view of primed-for-action male genitalia which her ladyship adored.

'You may as well *enjoy* this . . .' he repeated, his hand jerking hard on his cock, '. . . because you're going to be *raped*, no matter how much you protest.'

'Please, no,' she whispered – meaning please, yes – pussy wet, wishing she could get a finger to it and hoping that Wolfgang was not going to become so excited that he would again prematurely ejaculate.

'Suck me,' he hoarsely insisted, leaning forward to brush his glans over her cheek, then her lips. 'Suck my dick, Alexandra.'

'I'm not Alex . . .' she began, before her words were cut off and she forgot about this new fantasy of her being his dead wife as he shoved his cockhead against her teeth and she parted them to welcome it into her mouth.

Even as she fellated him with her customary relish for the act, Frannie, more needful by the second for that warm and fleshy pole in her pussy – oh, how wonderful at that moment had there been a second man so that she could enjoy a double penetration as had the wicked Suzy in the hologram! – was thinking, Don't come, don't come, please don't come yet.

She need not have been concerned – at least, not about that. For Wolfgang von Schwerin was coolly, utterly, insanely in control of himself. He intended to deliberately hold back his climax – which he knew from the unique, previous occasion like this would be the ultimate, mind-blowing experience – for he was evilly engaged in perpetrating on Frannie-Alexandra at that moment in his demented brain the heinous crime that he had the year before.

After a while he pulled out of Frannie's mouth.

Shaking with lust, he eased his body down hers until his cock was at her pussy, angled the glans in with one hand, and plunged.

Von Schwerin fucked trussed Frannie with pent-up fury, his heavy buttocks heaving with the speed of a pneumatic drill as he sucked on one of her nipples – as hard as if his mouth were a vacuum pump trying to draw milk – and feverishly kneaded her other breast. His free hand found its way beneath her buttocks, a finger penetrating her bottom hole.

Frannie climaxed. She climaxed again. Whilst wanting this glorious fuck never to end she was convinced that this frantic man would come any second. She was unable to see his face since it was buried in the pillow by the side of hers; imagining it to be contorted with approaching orgasm, and coming yet again herself, she awaited the explosion.

His backside stilled. Buried in her to the balls – but not ejaculating – he raised his face to stare at her.

Her world fell apart.

As her eyes went wide with fright, she began to mouth a scream; his expression was transformed to the hideous one of a demon. His face had turned a purplish hue. The ice-blue eyes bulged horribly, tiny red veins had appeared in them. More veins bulged on his forehead. His lips were curled into a fiendish snarl.

Von Schwerin's entire features had become a mask of terrifying, livid hate.

With Frannie's scream beginning to gather strength, he clamped his hand across her mouth.

Reaching over the edge of the bed he produced a dirty piece of rag from his dressing gown pocket; with it he firmly gagged fear-stricken Frannie.

'So, Alexandra,' he sneered. 'So. You thought you could come back to haunt me did you, you faithless, two-faced bitch? Well, the wild man of the mountain can come back too – just like the first time. He has climbed on to your balcony and broken into your room. And just like before, as he kills you – as he *cuts* you to death – he is going to have a fantastic orgasm!'

Until that moment, Frannie had been in total shock. Now, faced with death, she remembered her security ring; feeling for its emerald with the ball of her thumb, she found its edge and turned it against the spring.

Gregory, in his ground-floor room on the mountain side of the villa, is gently snoring, his huge chest peacefully rising and falling beneath a blanket. The screech from his bleeper – which lies on his bedside table – intrudes rudely on a childhood dream.

SAS-trained Gregory comes instantly awake and leaps from his bed.

With Frannie lying helpless and virtually paralysed with fear. Von Schwerin takes a knife from his dressing gown. It has an ancient, yellowing bone handle; its glinting edge is serrated and worn, there is a streaky brown stain on the blade. He menaces poor Frannie with it.

'The same knife as before, remember?' he slobbers. 'A woodsman's knife. The police failed to find it then, as they will do this time.' He flattens the blade on her breast as she tries to cringe right through the mattress. He frenziedly masturbates, panting, drooling, sliding the flat of the blade from one breast to the other.

Gregory takes the curving staircase two steps at a time, his striped pyjama jacket flapping behind him. He seeths with adrenalin, his bare feet thump, his onrushing weight shakes the stairs.

In his second-floor room, Adolf awakens. He listens for a moment, frowning. He rolls, naked, from his bed.

'*Now*, Alexandra. This time for good!' The sharp tip of the knife nicks Frannie's breast; she screams into the filthy rag.

A furious rattling of the doorknob. There is a tiny trickle of blood from Frannie's left breast but the knife, mercifully, bites no deeper. Von Schwerin's eyes spit venom over his shoulder; in his madness he jabbers incoherently. On the other side of the door, Gregory steps two paces back, measures his distance and charges. He hits the door so hard with his shoulder that his pyjama jacket rips. The metal lock splinters through the frame, the door smashes back into the wall – and Gregory's forward momentum carries him all the way to the bed where with a bellow of rage he seizes the Austrian's knife arm, yanks it clear of his mistress, up in the air and back over the man's head. Von Schwerin is violently flung in a clumsy backward roll to the floor; there is a fleshy tearing sound and a sharp crack as his arm is torn from its socket and at the same time snaps backwards at the elbow. The knife goes spinning through the air to clatter into a corner of the room.

The naked giant came rushing upon the scene with much the same velocity as had Gregory – who, trained to a high point of combat awareness by the SAS, had sensed his impending arrival.

Gregory met Adolf's charge with a short run of his own. Bullet head lowered, he caught the manservant a fearsome blow just beneath his ribs, knocking every vestige of breath from his body. There was a great, hissing gasp of pain from the man as he began to double over. Gregory, adrenalin continuing to churn within him, furious as a man could be, had not quite done with him; Adolf was folding forwards, Gregory was straightening up. Gregory's head made violent contact with the bottom of the giant's huge, square chin; there was the sickening sound of splintering bone as the chin disintegrated. Adolf, out cold, toppled sideways over the writhing, agonised form of his master.

'So,' grunted Gregory, barrel chest heaving beneath his open pyjama top as he grimly surveyed the heap of male naked flesh. 'So.'

He turned his attention to Frannie, running an eye which was perhaps more cynical than sympathetic over her nude body – which he had witnessed several times in the past, but only when Lady Ballington had been in serious trouble. He freed her, but he deliberately left the gag until the last – because the good Gregory wanted to have his 'ha'penny worth' whilst she was unable to interrupt him.

Uncharacteristically embarrassed and enormously relieved to have been saved from a most bloody death, Frannie scrambled a sheet up her body to cover her nakedness then reached behind her head for the knot in the rag as Gregory flatly observed, 'You were a *party* to bein' tied up then, your ladyship? Askin' for trouble, like, wasn't it?'

She frowned furiously at him as she struggled with the knot, her long nails hampering her. He came to her rescue. As he ungagged her she spluttered, 'Why do you assume that I *agreed* to it? Presumptuous of you, isn't it?'

'Dare say it is. But you would have bleeped me a darned sight earlier, wouldn't you, if you 'adn't been playing silly, dangerous *games*?'

'Thank you Gregory. I think that's quite *enough*.' Extremely grateful to him as she was, his moralising, as usual, niggled her.

He grunted an unintelligible reply as von Schwerin, trying in vain to heave his manservant off himself groaned, and whimpered, 'For pity's sake help me. Get a doctor.'

'A *doctor*?' A little of Gregory's anger returned. His eyes flickered from the Austrian, to the knife, and then to Frannie's tiny wound which she was dabbing with the edge of the sheet. 'What exactly was the bastard about to do to you?' he asked her.

'He, he threatened to hack me to death. He meant it.'

Gregory went and picked up the knife, then crouched down beside von Schwerin with it. 'I ought to cut your bleedin' balls off, you know that?' he snarled.

'No, don't, Gregory,' Frannie implored. She knew that it was well within his capacity to do so

– he had, once, those of a Dutch pervert in Los Angeles.*

'You get your*self* out from under, sunshine,' he said. 'And you can call yourself a doctor – whenever you get free.'

With the same bindings that had secured Frannie, as she climbed into her clothes he bound the painfully protesting von Schwerin's wrists to those of the unconscious manservant and his feet to Adolf's feet. Then he gagged them both. Lastly, he cut the telephone wires. He stuck his head into the corridor and listened; the house was asleep.

Frannie, dressed, was curious why he had trussed them.

'We don't need aggro with the Swiss police,' he told her. 'They're a real tough bunch and sunshine's a big cheese. They can work this one out when we're well clear of the country.'

'We leave now?'

'We do. We wake Matilda and we skedaddle as fast as we can.' He shook his head gravely at her, his expression one hundred per cent disapproval. 'It's about time you learned not to get yourself into these fuckin' fixes, it really is, Lady Ballington.'

She pulled a wry little, mildly irritated face at him. 'Gregory, I do *so* wish you wouldn't . . .' she shrugged. 'Oh, shit.'

'Wouldn't what, ma'am?'

She tutted. 'Never *mind.*'

Her eyes roved in disgust over the unseemly heap of male flesh; von Schwerin was groaning

* *Frannie.*

146

into his gag. His arm, turning a sickly shade of mauve, was swelling at the shoulder, lumpy and horribly twisted. Adolf's smashed chin hung slack and misshapen beneath the gag; blood dribbled down it.

'Let's, um, let's get the bloody *hell* out of here, shall we, Gregory?' said Frannie.

8

MAID IN HEAVEN

WE GOT OUR SKATES ON, I can tell you! – It was eleven fifteen when we left that grisly room and by just after eleven thirty, having dragged Matilda, bewildered and protesting, from her bed, we were roaring out through the gates of the Villa du Lac in a 'borrowed' Mercedes.

I navigated. We headed for Zurich airport, touching a hundred and eighty kilometres per hour on a wonderful road, and we were there in twenty minutes – not much slower than von Schwerin's helicopter had been on the way up.

But there was no convenient flight out of Zurich until morning. Fearing apprehension by the police if we hung around – and the subsequent tiresome and embarrassing interrogation – we high-tailed it out of there towards the border with Austria. Another forty minutes or so found us in the lakeside town of Rorschach – where we abandoned the Merc since we could hardly have risked taking it over the border. We crossed into Austria in a taxi to the Lake Constanz resort of Bregenz.

By one fifteen, highly relieved to be out of Switzerland, we were checking into the Hotel Constanz where I was obliged to share a suite with Matilda. . .

* * *

For the first time since losing herself in the carnal delights of being tied to a bed and pretend-ravished, followed by facing the ultimate horror of being a few knife slashes away from death, Frannie began to think coherently about what had transpired.

'I'm not so sure that we should have bolted, now that we have done,' she confided in Matilda as the two of them undressed for bed.

Matilda paused in the act of unclipping a bra, the way her elbows tilted forward with her hands behind her back exaggerating the size of her breasts. 'Of course we should, luvvy,' she said. 'We'd have been stuck there for ages. That bastard would have lied through his teeth about what really happened – and you have to take into consideration his power and influence.'

As Matilda's breasts tumbled free, Frannie stepped elegantly out of her knickers. The maid's eyes raked her mistress's naked loins speculatively; it had been quite some while since the two of them had been naked together – far too long, in Matilda's book.

'There is a certain something you don't know, though,' Frannie told her; she was also watching in rather more than casual interest as Matilda climbed out of her voluminous, white silk camiknickers to reveal her luxurious, black bush. 'I'll tell you all about it in bed.' She pursed her lips. 'I'm in desperate need of a bit of a cuddle.'

It was a cottage-style bedroom, over-fussy, with chintz curtains and tiny-flower print wallpaper – it would probably have been happier in a French hotel. But the lighting was low and comfortable and the bed large, soft and welcoming; in all, the room provided the sort of atmosphere that Frannie was in need of. Snuggled in Matilda's warm and fleshy arms, she related to her the story of the chilling murder of Wolfgang von Schwerin's wife the year before, how it had been attributed to a 'wild man of the woods' – and how she had been so terrifyingly furnished with the proof that the killer had been von Schwerin himself.

'So you see,' she concluded, her cheek nestled in Matilda's shoulder, 'we really should have stayed to face the hoo-hah, if only to make sure that the man is properly locked up.'

Matilda, as she covetously stroked Frannie's hair, considered the implications. 'It would be an awfully messy business,' she decided. 'The publicity would be unthinkably dreadful – a scandal to end all scandals. The bloody tabloids would have a field day. Can you imagine? "Lady Ballington forced to admit that she allowed sadistic killer to tie her to bed for sex." Too much, Fran. I mean, even his lordship would baulk at that, for all his sophistication.'

Frannie smiled. 'Victor? I doubt it. He'd probably take it as a huge joke.' Her hand wandered to Matilda's huge bosom, taking comfort in its silkiness. 'But Wolfgang might do it again, don't you see? Some other poor girl might be carved to death.'

'After what Gregory did to him and that horror story, Adolf? I should have thought he would have learned his lesson.'

'He's quite, quite mad, remember.'

'That's for sure.' Matilda planted a kiss on her forehead and pulled her tightly into herself; the conversation might be in deadly earnest, but that did not preclude the proximity of Frannie's nude body from exciting carnal need in her. 'You can't seriously be considering going back there?'

'I suppose not.'

'You didn't happen to have your video bag working last night?'

Frannie tilted her head to look into her eyes with a little frown. 'As a matter of fact I did. What are you suggesting?'

'Evidence?'

'You mean, hand the film·*over*? Expose myself to the leering eyes of half the Swiss police force? Out of the question, dear.'

'*Po*sitive evidence?'

'*Too* damned positive. Christ!'

Wrapped in the protective softness of one another's bodies, they were silently pensive for long moments. Frannie suddenly exclaimed, animatedly. 'The sound track. The video has a *sound* track. That's the *an*swer!'

'Is it?'

'Of course. He babbled the whole sick story to me. A complete confession. Then there's the recorded threat to murder me. I'll copy it and send it incognito to the police with an anonymous letter. They have voice-print techniques, don't they, which will prove it's him speaking? It should do the trick. I'll see to it as soon as we get home.'

Matilda's fingers gentled her cheek. 'Not bad.'

'I feel happier now. I was beginning to feel that I'd be a sort of accomplice if I kept what I know to myself.' Her lips found Matilda's and they kissed for long seconds, mutual passion steadily rising. Then Frannie said, quietly, 'I worry about myself, you know.'

'You do? That's new.'

'No it's not. I know I've mentioned it before. My sex adventures so often go hand in hand with trouble, with danger. You don't suppose that . . .' she gazed doubtfully up into Matilda's eyes. '. . . God, no, that's a pretty bloody silly idea, isn't it?'

'I'm not a mind reader.'

'It was occurring to me that perhaps what I get up to sometimes is so wicked that I get punished for it? Divine retribution, something like that?'

Matilda shook her head, a smile dimpling her cheek. 'And sometimes you're a child. You can't help that you're highly sexed, that you get the hots for one man after the other. . .'

'And woman,' Frannie interrupted.

'And woman after the other. And because you happen to be beautiful, because you positively radiate sex, you succeed where others less fortunate can only helplessly lust. You're very rich, you're – forgive me – spoilt. And you're dead lucky, my love.'

'Yes, but – excess? Is that right?'

'First we need to understand what exactly excess is. I'll tell you. Excess is indulging in an

152

appetite – eating, drinking, sex, whatever – over and above its normal requirements. Excess is making yourself ill with your indulgence. You don't do that.'

'I always seem to have room for more sex.'

Matilda chuckled. 'There you are then. It ain't excess, darling – it's a ravenous, healthy appetite, and that you can hardly help. Indulge, say I. Take pleasure, give pleasure. Do no actual harm, commit no actual physical sin, and where *is* the harm?'

'You're so good for me, Matilda, you know that? Thank you.'

'You want me to be even more good for you?' Matilda's hand crawled up the back of Frannie's thigh as her voice dropped to a whisper.

Frannie nuzzled Matilda's breasts and briefly sucked on a nipple. 'Let's be good for each *other*?'

'We are, Fran. We always are.'

The end of words. Lips find lips, tongues mingle as loving fingers seek out furry, fleshy objectives. A quickening of warm and sweet breath into one another's mouths. Discovery; the fingers eager, trembling against pussy lips, parting them, intruding into tight moistness as thumbs gentle clitorises. Both women very sure of themselves, totally aware of what their bodies require of one another.

However, there is a craving within them for more than just sex; this is lovemaking, they need love – Frannie because she wants the comfort of it, Matilda because she has in any case been in love with her mistress for as long as she can remember.

Passion rises. Frannie rolls on top of Matilda, sinking gratefully into the chubby, yielding flesh, grinding her pubis. Her fingers are now deep inside Matilda's pussy – as Matilda's are in hers – and as they move them in long, urgent strokes the sides of their hands brush and knock together.

Matilda's free hand gropes Frannie's rocking behind, the stubby fingertips slide into its cleft, one finds the tiny bottom hole and intrudes to the first knuckle.

'Othello?' Matilda gasps into Frannie's mouth. 'Would you like me to get Othello?'

But Frannie has no need of, or desire for, the artificiality of a dildo at this moment, she craves only naked, acquiescent female flesh – Matilda's flesh – and she murmurs, 'No. Just love me.'

So they love.

Even when Frannie swivels around on Matilda to wrap her thighs around Matilda's face and examine the open, copiously bushed pussy beneath her nose before plunging her fingers there yet again – it is love. As she dips her head to replace her fingers with her tongue while at the same time Matilda's tongue first licks, then eases its salivary way into her cunt – it is love.

It is, of course, sex. It is heavy, steaming, panting, gasping, juicy sex – but it is also love, lesbian love at its most compelling. They are not simply eating pussy, these two ardent, needful ladies, they are loving each other through familiar, adored parts of their anatomies – and it could never be quite the same for either of them with another female.

Their bodies exquisitely attuned on this night of

nights, they shudder and sigh through perfectly mutual orgasms, thighs clamping luxuriously around one another's ears, toes curling, hands screwing the bed linen. They lie still for long seconds – except for their tongues which continue to lazily lick the oozing sweetness as they moan and mewl in pleasure.

Frannie reverses position on Matilda. Pubis idly rocks against pubis, damp bushes pleasantly mingling.

They kiss. Tongue meets tongue to form a thin cocktail of pussy juice residue and saliva between them – a nectareous taste most special.

'I don't know why I bother with men,' Frannie, deliciously content, murmurs.

'Oh, but I do,' Matilda throatily responds.

'Why?'

'Cock,' Matilda tells her. They laugh dirtily – and most happily – together.

9

ROCKING THE BOAT

WHEN SHE AWOKE NEXT TO Matilda the following morning, Frannie could hardly believe that it was only Monday; behind her were five days so packed with sex, adventure and travel that they might have occupied a month.

With Matilda making mumbling noises as she began to wake up, Frannie consulted her Orient Express timetable; if they could somehow manage to get to Venice that day it would leave Tuesday clear to enjoy the city before their departure, as arranged, on the train with Neville Duke and the ravishing Sandra on Wednesday morning.

After breakfast they discovered that the closest direct flight to Venice was from Innsbruck; there was no alternative but to take a taxi the hundred and fifty kilometres to that city. Frannie, naturally, would have preferred to order the Ballington family Lear to the nearest small airport which could accommodate it – probably over the border in Germany at Wangen – but Victor, annoyingly, happened to be using it that day.

They arrived, late in the afternoon, at Venice's world famous Gritti Palace hotel – one-time home to the chief magistrate Andrea Gritti in the fifteenth century – where they met up with Neville and Sandra.

Neville was relaxed, lightly tanned – there had been several days of unbroken sunshine throughout Italy – and in generally fine form. Matilda decided to take a siesta and Sandra went shopping, leaving him and Frannie alone together in the palatial hotel lounge where a fabulous chandelier swooped spectacularly from a shimmering ornamental ceiling.

Europe, Neville declared, had been just great for him. As they chatted, Frannie found herself thinking about her sexual romp with him and Victor in the ruined mill at Stratton, and then about the wonderful three-way swing they had enjoyed with Sandra in Paris. She mused that the last time she had seen the American had been when she had discovered him naked in Matilda's sleeping car on the Orient Express at six o'clock in the morning. Studying his handsome face with its dark; amazingly long-lashed eyes – as he told her about his discovery of the overwhelmingly beautiful city of Venice – she found her heart fluttering as her mind became filled with thoughts of more sex with him. As soon as the opportunity arose, she used Matilda to steer the conversation around to the subject.

'Cuddlesome, is she not, my maid?' she suddenly asked, her words dripping innuendo.

The unexpected question failed to ruffle his smooth urbanity. 'I guess nobody should know better than you,' he coolly told her.

'What makes you think that?'

'She introduced me to Othello.' He said the

words with the American tendency of turning a statement into a question.

'Shit. Of course, she just would do something like that.' She paused, mouthing a smile. 'I suppose you two passed a really raunchy night together?'

'You could say that. Say, how come she's your maid, and your friend, and your lover? How does that work?'

Frannie toyed with her martini as she said, 'She should never have been in service, poor love. She comes from a very upper-class family which went utterly skint like so many. The reverse of me, actually. I came from a fairly skint family and got lucky by marrying Victor.'

'Victor was the lucky one.' His eyes went on a brief tour of her breasts; braless, they juttled temptingly through a simple, canary-yellow blouse, their nipples offering shadowy promise. His eyes latched on to hers. 'Skint? I take it that means broke?'

'Right. In the case of Matilda's family, crippled by the cost of trying to keep up an ancestral home. She's actually more part of the family than a maid. My paid, personal companion.'

'Not to mention enthusiastic lover?'

'When the mood takes us.'

'She's one hell of a sight with that black dildo in place. I tell you, I've never seen anything quite like it.'

Frannie gaped at him. 'She put it *on* for you, for Christ's sake?'

'I kinda persuaded her. Unbelievable. All that succulent white flesh and that great, black cock sticking straight out between her legs. Something else!'

'The shameless bloody hussy!'

He grinned. 'You bet. That's the way I like them.' His hand found her white-skirted knee. 'You're not so very shy and retiring yourself.'

'And just what is that supposed to mean?'

'It means – heh, do you still fancy me?' The hand gentled.

'Maybe. But I rather gathered you now prefer my maid?'

'She made for an interesting diversion. Prefer? Impossible.'

'What about Sandra?'

He shrugged. 'Great chick. Good-time girl. But like your Matilda, she's my travelling companion. I dig variety. And I find you . . .', he studied her, '. . . more, challenging – you get my drift?'

'No. What are you driving at, mister?'

'Waiting for you to show up, whilst taking a trip in a gondola on the Grand Canal out there, I had a great idea for a dare. Sandra's a marvellous chick, like I said, but I mentioned it to her and she just doesn't have the balls.' His hand slipped a short way up her thigh, under the skirt. 'You fancy doing something just a little different, later on, after dinner?'

'Is it sex?'

'You bet your life it's sex. And how!'

She sipped her martini, eyes smokily on his, excitement stirring in her belly. 'So tell me about it. Shoot.'

He did, as her eyes widened a little more with each word. When he finished she laughed incredulously. 'You're out of your tiny mind,' she told him.

'Aren't you a little nuts, too? Somewhat of a sex maniac?'

She produced a twisted, wonderfully wicked little grin. 'Only most of the time. So let's do it, lover boy!'

* * *

During a candlelit dinner in the Hotel Gritti Palace's famous Club de Doge restaurant – on a terrace directly overlooking the serene, dark waters of the Grand Canal – Frannie, slightly nervous about what she had agreed to do, found herself frequently watching the slowly passing boats and gondolas as she speculated on how it was going to be later. Many times when she returned her attention to the sumptuously spread table she caught either Sandra or Neville – and sometimes the two of them – regarding her with enigmatic little smiles: Matilda had not been let in on the secret.

At her slinkiest and most desirable, Sandra was poured into a black crepe evening dress; her few accessories – a silk choker with its ends draped together forwards over one bared shoulder, a chunky, multiple-banded bead bracelet, the shoes, a single headband topping her burgundy curls – were also black, with the exception of a startlingly bright, diamond cluster broach. The overall effect – combined with the fact that she was gently tanned and wearing no noticeable make-up – enhanced the entrancing glitter of her pale jade, almost luminous eyes. Every time she looked at the girl, Frannie lusted to have her once again naked in her arms; she could not imagine – and this despite the fact that she was certainly vain enough to know how exceptionally lovely she herself was – how the American playboy could want to be with any other woman.

The atmosphere at the little dinner party was a rare one – and not simply because the group of three women and a man was off balance. It had to do with the fact that Neville had had ribald carnal knowledge of all three women and that Sandra and Frannie madly – and obviously – fancied one another even though they were both keenly aware that the imminent item on the sexual menu concerned Frannie and Neville.

Matilda, meanwhile – dining in the company of the man who had proved to be the fuck of her dreams – was being clumsily awkward, refusing, naturally, to wear her spectacles; she twice managed to knock over her wine. In her nervousness with Neville sitting next to her she was mostly silent, and she stammered every time she was brought into the conversation.

Finally the moment arrived. Pushing aside his coffee cup, Neville got to his feet. He excused himself to Sandra and Matilda and suggested that he and Frannie got changed; he would meet her in the foyer.

Frannie had drunk just enough to calm her jitters and to heighten her anticipatory excitement. In her suite she speedily changed from her silver lamé evening dress into Neville's suggested ensemble – a thin, summer sweater, a loose, pleated, knee-length skirt, crotchless tights – but no knickers – and flat shoes.

In the foyer, for some idiotic reason she felt shamelessly exposed without her knickers – as if everyone was peering under her skirt. Neville appeared seconds after her, in designer jeans and a white T-shirt emblazoned with the famous name and logo of the Jockey Club.

At first glance the American's especially chartered gondola, which bobbed gently at the Gritti Palace's private quay, looked much like any other. Then Frannie noticed as he stepped aboard, making the fragile craft rock, that the sunshade canvases, normally furled at night around their crooked wooden poles, were spread from pole to pole – not arranged horizontally as in the daytime to provide a patch of shade, but vertically so as to completely obscure the boatman's view of his passengers.

Neville held out his hand and helped Frannie aboard; water slopped against the low gunwales. The gondolier – as ordered by Neville – had procured extra cushions; Frannie was obliged to step on to one, for the area between the single-backed upholstered seat with the canvas sheet stretched behind it, and the traditionally ornamental, elegantly carved prow of the boat, was filled with soft, maroon cushions.

'We'll just sit quietly for a while,' said Neville, taking her hand. The two of them made themselves comfortable on the seat as the gondolier cast off and began to punt them into the centre of the canal.

Above them, as Sandra and Matilda sipped

liqueurs with their second coffees, Sandra said, 'Why you do not put on your glasses?'

'What? Why?' mumbled Matilda.

'There is something maybe you would like to see, no?'

'No? Oh, all right.' She scrabbled in her bag, found her bifocals and fumbled them on to her nose.

Convinced that Neville and Frannie had gone off for a sly quickie, ruing her lot – for she would have given anything for another tumble with the American herself – Matilda was surprised to see them in the gondola. They were kissing. As the boat approached the centre of the canal Neville's hand, the action visible even at that distance and in the gloom, began to grope beneath Frannie's russet sweater.

'Golly,' Matilda exclaimed, blinking astonishment.

Snuggling tightly into Neville as his hand encircled her bare breast and he toyed with its responsive nipple, Frannie muttered – into his mouth – 'People will notice.'

'What people?' He was right, there were few boats, none of them close by. 'In any case, let them – it's part of the thrill.'

'But I don't see how we're going to actually . . .'

He cut off her question by crushing his lips on to hers. Then he whispered, as he shifted his hand to her other breast, 'But we're going to.'

She shuddered. 'Yes, we are, aren't we?'

'I've got a stalk-on just thinking about it. Feel me up.'

Her pink-nailed hand dropped to his crotch.

Beneath the denim his sturdy erect cock strained sideways across the top of his thigh. She folded her palm over it and rubbed. 'Nice. I want it.'

'And have it you shall.' He gave her breast an extra hard squeeze then slipped his hand out from under her sweater. 'Come.'

With great caution, taking care not to rock the craft too alarmingly, they lay down amongst the cushions, facing each other, heads to the prow.

On the restaurant terrace, Matilda and Sandra were keenly watching as the gondola stopped rocking; it was punted slowly away until the figures were no longer distinguishable. 'They seem to have deserted us,' observed Matilda, '. . . the dirty, lucky, randy sods!'

'Sods? What is this sods?' asked Sandra.

'I suppose literally it's short for sodomites.'

'Ah. *This* I know. Sodomy. The cock up the backside, no?' chirruped Sandra with charming artlessness.

Matilda could not help laughing at her. 'That's the sort of thing, right,' she said jollily.

'But I think, not on the boat, no?'

'Bloody *hell*, no!'

Sandra gazed into the distance at the now toy-sized gondola. 'In a little while they come back past here – then we shall be seeing.'

'Seeing what?'

'You must wait.' Sandra's eyes returned from the canal to rove over Matilda's copious bosom. 'You have the lovely big tits,' she murmured. 'Me, I ad*ore* the big tits.'

Matilda's spirits soared along with her libido. '*Do* you now dear?' she purred. 'How very nice!'

The illumination in the middle of Venice's Grand Canal at ten thirty at night was hardly of the brightness of the Blackpool, England, variety, but it was enough for anyone with sharp eyesight to have had some idea of what Frannie and Neville were up to – even from the banks or the buildings, but most especially from any closely passing boat. The idea – of course – was to fuck with that in mind and not to make such an obvious display of it that their actions would land them in police cells for the night.

The actual screwing was yet to begin; each of their moves towards this objective was stealthy and discreet – and that much more arousing because of the need for prudence. They were close together on their cushioned water-bed. As the gondola slipped along on its almost silent way between the lit-up, elegant and beautiful palazzi lining the canal – great houses of the fifteenth and sixteenth century of which there were some two hundred along the banks – Frannie lifted a knee to rest it high on the side of Neville's thigh. She spread the material of her tawny coloured skirt over his hip; beneath its cover, as he lay very still, not, at that moment, touching her, she undid his gold buckled belt and one by one popped open the metal buttons of his jeans. Of its own accord, as she dealt with the bottom button, his cock, unrestrained by underpants, sprang free.

Neville's solid phallus felt hot and throbbing and, unseen but nestling in her hand, incredibly exciting. He grunted with pleasure as, slowly, enjoying the sensuously silken feel of its thinly stretched skin, she slid her palm softly up and down it.

Climbing up her nylon-covered thigh, Neville's hand did not stop until it encountered warm, naked flesh where the crotch was cut away; she had not actually had a pair of crotchless tights in her luggage, she had done the job herself with nail scissors and the edges were fraying. Flattening his hand beneath her, between her legs, he took hold of her pussy as if cradling a small, furry animal. As the tip of his finger penetrated her wetness she responded by jerking hard on his cock and pushing her knee further across him; several inches of her thigh were now whitely free of her skirt.

'Ready then,' he muttered. 'Good and wet and ready.'

'And you. Good and *hard* and ready.' Her spare hand seized his balls. With her eyes on his chest in the remaining gap between their torsos, reading his T-shirt motif, she whispered, 'So why don't you ride me, Mister Jockey?'

He moved with exquisite slowness, pushing his hips into her as she guided his cock on its way whilst continuing to wank him until its head was comfortably lodged inside her pussy.

'Come *on*, baby,' Frannie urged, squeezing his balls, tingling with excitement, '. . . *fuck* me.'

'Yeah, but gently,' he said, easing his prick up her fraction by fraction. 'You wanna rock the boat?'

She produced a throaty, dirty giggle. 'Yes, I want to rock the fucking boat.'

Over his shoulder, Frannie, but dimly aware of it, watched the illuminated walls of a breathtakingly beautiful palace as they slid quietly past it;

in puce-coloured stone, they were covered with windows of white stone and marble, and arched and curlicued balconies. From a verandah hovering just above the level of the canal drifted strains of Chopin. A couple leaning over its balustraded wall were gazing in interest at the solitary gondola with its lovingly embracing passengers.

When his cock was planted in Frannie's pussy to its base and the open fronts of his jeans were pressed hard into her tights-covered thighs, Neville held still. 'I guess we made it,' he murmured.

'Not yet, we didn't.'

Frannie wriggled her bottom; she felt deliciously, wickedly horny, thus impaled in full view – if only they had been aware of the fact – of perhaps a hundred or more people. The gondola bobbed only fractionally, but the movement proved sufficient to produce arousing friction between their cosily locked genitals. She squirmed her backside some more, beginning to get into a just perceptible rhythm. 'You think we can get off like this?' she whispered.

'Uhuh. But why the hurry?' Raising his voice he asked the gondolier to turn his craft around and head back the way they had come.

The man obliged without a murmur – but risking a quick peek around the tarpaulin as he did so. His ageing, black eyes narrowed at what he saw – a clearly highly sexual embrace between two very switched-on passengers. Smiling to himself he went back to his job of punting his love-boat.

Since the environment precluded vigorous fucking, hands got exceptionally busy; Frannie cupped and fondled Neville's hairy balls whilst rubbing her erect little clitoris and Neville succeeded in intruding the index finger of one hand into her bottom hole and that of the other in her pussy, crammed against his cock. 'Talk dirty to me,' muttered Frannie, heart beginning to wildly thump, finding it most difficult to restrain her backside from jerking hard.

'About?' His voice was the husky one of a man well on his way towards orgasm.

'About Matilda. About fucking Matilda. About tanning her arse.'

'Matilda has a gorgeous fat white butt. I strapped it with my belt until it was rosy red. She loved it.'

'That's it. That's what I want to hear, you fucking pervert.' Frannie poked her tongue inside his mouth, mingling her saliva with his and licking all around the insides of his lips. Then she whispered, 'Did you fuck it?'

'Yeah. I gave her the screwing of her life.' He was beginning to pant his words.

'No, did you fuck *it*? Did you fuck her arsehole? Did you *bugger* my maid, you filthy *sod*?' She was relishing talking in this way; it almost compensated in terms of arousal for the necessity of restrained movement.

'I buggered her, yeah. I squeezed my dick all the way up her tiny bumhole,' he gasped. 'It was, it was real *tight*, you know? A tight, tiny hole in a big, fat butt.'

Neville was speaking in a series of fractured

grunts, he was unable to keep from jerking his hips in response to her wriggles; the boat was beginning to rock. But seeing that they were approaching the Gritti Palace Hotel, he somehow had the presence of mind to remember a promise he had made to Sandra. He began to roll Frannie on to her back.

'What are you doing?' she muttered.

'Don't for Christ's sake lift your knees.' He was on top of her now, his weight bearing her down amongst the cushions. He contrived to pull her skirt half down each outside of her thighs so that it would not be completely obvious to an onlooker that its front middle was rucked up above her belly. 'How close are you to coming?' he panted.

'Very.' She heaved her bottom beneath him. 'I'm almost there. Fuck me properly, *please*? *Fuck me.*'

Pressing his mouth over hers, he risked the first of what were to be three fiercely climactical jerks.

Matilda could not credit the evidence of her own eyes. 'They're not ... God, I mean they're not ... they *can't* be?' she exclaimed as the rocking gondola was slowly punted past the prestigious Club de Doge restaurant.

Sandra's eyes were shining. 'I knew he would,' she said, 'I *knew* it. What did I tell you? They are fucking.'

Which happened to be the precise moment when they ceased the activity. Even as Neville's orgasm began to grip him – a time when he would in normal circumstances ram it in and out of his woman with all his power – he stilled, letting his unstoppable seed well up from his balls to fill

Frannie's climactically contracting vagina. They came superbly together, grunting their way through the experience into one another's mouths, then relaxing little by little as the Gritti Palace Hotel slipped slowly behind them.

After a while they simultaneously managed a lethargic laugh of triumph.

'We did it, honey,' said Neville, as his cock wilted within her. 'We fucking *made* it!'

'Didn't we just?' Frannie giggled. 'So how about we now go for a little sightseeing ride in a gondola?'

A minute or so earlier, the boatman, slightly alarmed by the sudden near-violent rocking of his craft, had again peered around the canvas partition; what he had pruriently observed in those few climactic seconds had brought a grin to his gnarled face which was even now only just beginning to dissolve.

On the restaurant balcony, Sandra rested both her hands on the backs of those of still-shocked Matilda. She smiled into her eyes. 'I am believing that it is perhaps our turn now, is it not?' she huskily said. 'Shall we go to your room, no? I would very much like to meet this famous Othello of yours. We *are* in Venice, after all.'

10

DESDEMONA'S DICK!

RARELY HAD MATILDA HAD THE opportunity to sport with one of Frannie's lovers, and never before to also get it together with that lover's girlfriend. As soon as she locked her bedroom door on them, Matilda folded Sandra into her arms and kissed her on the lips ardently; the German girl tasted of cherry brandy which flavour mingled interestingly with the creme de menthe tinting the tip of Matilda's tongue light green. Sandra responded with panting enthusiàsm, rolling her full tits into Matilda's bosom, grinding her flat belly into the maid's plumpness, squeezing her fat bottom with scarlet-nailed hands.

Playing the male part, Matilda took charge of the proceedings; as they embraced, she ambled Sandra backwards to the antique, canopied bed, then tumbled her on to it. As her legs splayed, the black crepe of her dress stretched so alarmingly it appeared to be about to split. Muttering, 'Let me get you out of this,' she first removed the choker then fumbled around for a zipper, discovering its little, metal tag under Sandra's uncovered armpit. Only when she moved her face in close as she tugged at it did Matilda become aware of the thin reddish fuzz there.

'You don't shave under your arms?' she observed, surprised.

'You like, darlink?' the girl responded, flinging her arm dramatically back above her head.

Matilda had rarely encountered this phenomenon in a woman. As she eased the zipper down to Sandra's hips she studied the tuft of hair, eyes inches from it. 'I think I do,' she decided.

'I hope so. Many Germans – and other Continentals neither – do not shave there. The French womans, they never do. They know it has the scent of sex. Cassolette, is called by the French. You English, you know not about these things.'

Matilda shoved her nose into the fuzzy armpit and nuzzled. Unperfumed, it had a not unpleasant, musky aroma. 'It's rather . . . nice,' she muttered. She lifted her face to kiss Sandra tenderly on the lips. 'Nevertheless,' she huskily told her, '. . . we English can probably teach you foreigners a thing or two when it comes to the sack.'

'Sack?'

'Bed. Sex.'

'Then teach me.' She pulled the single shoulder of her dress down over her elbow and slipped her arm out of it, then dragged the bodice to her waist to bare her exquisite breasts; they trembled deliciously as she did so. 'My body is your body, *mein schatz*. Be doing whatever you wish with it.'

This blatant invitation had Matilda almost shaking with desire; a knot started in her throat which she swallowed away. As Sandra coquettishly raised her hips from the bed, she eased the dress over them, failing to hold her over-eager hands quite steady. When the material was halfway down the girl's thighs, Matilda, stooping close the better to focus on what was revealed, gasped; black stockings clung most sensuously to slender, perfect legs – and she was wearing neither suspender belt nor panties. But what truly delighted and amazed Matilda, quickening her pulse, setting her belly on fire, was the fact that Sandra's copper-haired pussy was surrounded by colourful butterflies, five of them with wings spread, one tucked into each thigh top, three hovering between belly and bush.

Sandra chuckled throatily. 'What do you think?'

Matilda ran an intrigued finger over a Red Admiral which appeared to be fluttering from pussy to navel. 'They're beautiful.'

'Transfers. I put different transfers, often, in secret places. Is making the sex more fun, yes? You like?'

'I like.' Matilda's pudgy fingers crept down amongst the crinkly pubic hairs. 'Maybe I can't teach you anything after all.'

'No? *Ja*, sure you can. You can teach me about Othello. But first I am wanting to see *your* tits.'

Matilda had on a peach-coloured taffeta evening dress which buttoned down the front. She was squatting on her haunches with her face bent low over Sandra's belly and Sandra had only slightly to raise her hands to get at the buttons; when they were undone she fumbled open the hooks in the front of Matilda's simple white bra and her big breasts tumbled free into her hands.

'Nice,' mumbled Sandra, squashing and rolling

them together. 'Why do you not rub them on mine?'

Shifting her weight so that she was astride the girl's knees, Matilda swooped. Their breasts met, Matilda's heavily wobbling as she jiggled her torso from side to side. Nipples brushed nipples, tongues found tongues. Taffeta rustled as Sandra's hands dived beneath Matilda's skirt and ran up her bare, plump calves to find their way under her knickers and cling to her buttocks, hooking greedily into the plenteous flesh.

'I do like this to you when you fuck me with Othello,' Sandra murmured into Matilda's mouth.

'I'll get him. It.'

Feeling slightly disorientated, not quite able to believe that this amazingly gorgeous specimen of youthful pulchritude was – except for stockings and shoes and transfers and her chunky bead bracelet – naked on her bed and craving for a dildo fuck, Matilda swung off her to stand on Chinese rug at the foot of the bed where she kicked off her shoes and climbed out of her clothes.

Sandra's eyes travelled appreciatively over Matilda's stupendous white curves, then lingered on the heavy black thatch between her legs. She wetted her lips. 'I *like*,' she breathed, as her hand stole to her pussy.

Buttock flesh wobbling, Matilda padded to a closet; the stripes on her bottom from her strapping had not quite faded away. As Matilda fished in a suitcase for the dildo, Sandra asked, 'Who is it who has been beating your bum?'

'What?' Matilda looked over her shoulder to

examine herself in a mirror on the inside of the closet door. 'Oh. Right.' She turned back towards the bed, black rubber phallus in hand. 'Your bloody kinky boyfriend, that's who!'

'*Ja*? At such things he is very *goot.*'

Matilda grinned. 'I'll say!'

Her grin gradually changed into an expression of almost wolfish lust as Matilda approached the bed – where Sandra had parted her thighs and was toying with her pussy with two fingers.

'*Mein Gott,*' exclaimed Sandra, her eyes latching widely onto Othello with its dangling velvet straps, '. . . this is some plenty big thing, no?'

'Plenty big enough for *you*, dear.'

Matilda began to strap the dildo in place. The mere doing of this brought upon her a feeling of almost macho maleness quite unlike that of donning it to satisfy Neville's prurient curiosity; that had been just plain, wanton exhibitionism. Now she was about to put it to the bawdy use for which it was intended, and the butch within her was lured most lustily out. With Othello in place as if it had actually grown there between her legs, and her right hand gripping it, she descended upon the eager and ready Sandra. Kneeling between the girl's splayed legs and raised knees she sat on her haunches, bending forward so that her tits and stomach were squashed into her thighs and, with the dildo digging into the bed, she lapped Sandra's pussy like a cat at a saucer of milk.

Sandra groaned as if in pain. Lifting her feet up she crossed them on Matilda's back as the experienced tongue went busily to work; it began by flickering, teasing, exploring, then it rooted inside her vagina as far as it would stretch. Cupping the girl's taut buttocks, Matilda raised them from the bed – as if by so doing she could open up that sweet, copper-haired cunt even wider to her mouth.

After minutes of this Sandra was so turned on, so wet, she was unable to take any more. Her heels drummed impatiently on Matilda's well-padded spine. Rolling her head from side to side, her eyes tightly closed, her hands screwing into the maid's hair, she panted, '*Fick* me. *Fick* me, please *fick* me, Matilda!'

Matilda's German was not so non-existent to cause her to miss the meaning of *that* little word. She treated the girl's clitoris to a final, avid little suck, and straightened up. Sandra's legs trailed up her back and over her shoulders, until her feet were resting on her shoulders and her calves crammed into her tits. The girl was on her back with her legs almost straight up in the air and her buttocks tucked between Matilda's thighs and belly, her spine curved off the bed; for a moment the dildo rudely rested up over Sandra's parted pussy lips – the balls tucked under her pussy, the beautifully moulded glans pressing into the butterfly below her navel.

Thus Matilda commenced to fuck Sandra; lifting her bottom with one hand, she introduced the head of the artificial cock with the other, lowering the moaning German on to it until she was fully impaled. She took a good, meaty grip of her buttocks and began to steadily raise and lower them, eyes feasting on the thick length of black rubber as, glistening with vaginal secretions, it poled the delectable butterfly-surrounded teutonic cunt.

Matilda metamorphosed into the formidable fucking machine she could, at times – to Frannie's delight – be. After a while she tired of bouncing Sandra's buttocks up and down – besides, with her legs closed as they were the dildo itself was hardly moving so its clever extensions behind were doing very little to stimulate her clitoris and pussy. She contrived herself on top of Sandra without uncoupling and began to screw her vigorously in the missionary position. As she heaved away she ardently kissed her lips, her weight firmly on her elbows like any solicitous male lover, her tits dangling over Sandra's and bouncing on them, her bottom – with its velvet strapped cleft and its fading red stripes – wobbling and trembling.

Content to lie beneath her and let Matilda make all the action, with her hands fiercely clinging to Matilda's bouncing behind, Sandra mewled and shrieked her way through a string of orgasms while her hermaphroditic partner – feeling more man than woman – relentlessly banged herself towards what was destined to be a single, explosive climax.

Had the rubber testicles been real, they would surely have spilled a formidable load; for when Matilda – aroused beyond measure from fucking the stupendously sexy body beneath her, by the ribald sight of her black prick slamming in and out of a copper-haired butterfly-surrounded cunt, by the constant sensuous tit contact, by the girl's gluttonous sexual noises, and by Othello's ingenious extensions – at last reached orgasm herself, it swept through her with the unstoppable impact of a tidal wave.

She bared her teeth, she closed her eyes, she gave a final heave so strong it shifted Sandra inches up the bed, her body – as far as its shuddering layers of fat would allow – went rigid, and she let loose a sound which was something between a howl and a sob. Then slowly, very slowly, she relaxed, rolling over on to her side and taking the replete Sandra with her to lie in an intimate unmoving embrace.

When their perspiration had dried, when their breathing was back to normal, when their pulse rates had steadied, they opened their eyes almost simultaneously.

Sandra lazily smiled. Her hand crept down between their bodies until its fingers met with two inches of the base of the dildo, the rest of which remained buried in her very wet, most contented pussy.

'I fucking adore this Othello of yours,' she drawled. 'A huge black dick which *never* goes *down*? This is a paradise, no? . . . No?'

11

INTERNATIONAL RELATIONS

TUESDAY AFTERNOON FOUND FRANNIE AND Neville Duke enjoying a game of backgammon on the Gritti Palace hotel terrace. As a player Frannie was just a little above average. The American was extremely good. He was a friend of a world authority on the game – and ex-world champion – Paul Magriel, who had been his mentor. However, despite the fact that the closest Frannie had been to an expert player was to read the renowned Magriel book on the subject, she was getting all the right dice and was way ahead.

It was a most pleasant way to pass an afternoon, there in Venice on the lazy Grand Canal, shaded from the almost hot sunshine, fanned by a gentle breeze and with boats and gondolas slipping quietly by. The balmy atmosphere seemed to be somehow contributing to Frannie's marvellous dice; in an almost certain losing position with four men left in her home board spread between her one and six point whilst Neville had only three on his one and two points, crazy gambler that she was prone to be, she accepted an untakeable double from four to eight and then, after Neville got two men off, proceeded to roll her only possible winning number – a double six.

She laughed triumphantly as Neville – who took his game most seriously – silently fumed whilst writing down the score.

From above them a deep pleasant voice said, 'I once heard Joe Dwek say that if you can't do that you shouldn't be playing backgammon.'

Frannie, who had been vaguely aware for some time that a man had been standing near their table watching the game, glanced at him; he was stocky, short and dark with an interesting, slightly babyish face. She flashed him a friendly smile. 'Forgive my ignorance, but who is Joe Dwek?'

'One of the world's greatest players,' said Neville. Then he added, irritably, 'And he was bullshitting, of course.'

Frannie fluttered her eyelashes and shrugged. 'But I won, didn't I?'

'You should never have taken the damned double.' He managed a feeble grin. 'Yeah, you won.' He asked the stranger if he was a player, and the man accepted his invitation to join them in a chouette.

The newcomers' skill became immediately apparent; he played with a speed and fluidity which was impressive, hardly seeming to think after his dice came to rest before moving his pieces. He was wearing an open-necked, cream silk shirt displaying a very hairy chest on which rested a thin gold chain with a small gold coin. On his perfectly manicured fingers he had two simple gold rings, on one wrist an antique gold watch chain and on the other a square-faced Cartier watch with a black crocodile strap; a subtle declaration of wealth.

Frannie liked his style, his easy charm and boyish smile. As he started scoring points against them with a run in the box she decided he was most agreeable, every inch the gentleman.

They finished the game an hour and a half later with Frannie, despite her formidable adversaries, an equal winner with their new friend. With grudging good humour Neville paid out three hundred and twenty dollars in cash to each of them; he had managed to lose thirty two points at twenty dollars a point.

Over cocktails they discovered he was an Italian. His name was Giovanni de Cotta, he was from Florence, a businessman; he was vague about what sort of business. Frannie was not exactly getting the hots for him but – as almost always – she was sexually curious. When she mentioned that they were leaving on the Orient Express in the morning he wished them a pleasant trip and then, shortly afterwards, he departed.

Frannie promptly forgot about Mr de Cotta, but at ten fifteen in the morning there he was, at Santa Lucia Station, boarding the train. He was most affable, cracking a joke about deciding to take the express because he needed to relieve Neville of more of his money – to which challenge the American naturally rose; by mid afternoon the two of them were engaged in such a tremendous battle that they paid no attention to the spectacular scenery as the train crossed the massive terraced Brenner Pass on its way through the Alps into Austria.

By tea-time, as they reached the lovely River Inn and the outskirts of Innsbruck at the foot of the pass – the Garden of Europe – the score in the backgammon tussle had remarkably levelled out at zero – which was an ideal moment for Frannie and Sandra to join in.

How the delectable Sandra managed to be the only winner fell into the category of one of those occasional incredible happenings in what Jacoby – perhaps the greatest authority on backgammon – has described as the 'cruellest game'. She was little more than a beginner, understanding only the basic elements of the game. Yet she had a run in the box – that is to say playing against the other three with each of them taking it in turns to play for the team – of seventeen consecutive games, in the process piling up over a hundred points. It was unbelievable, like magic, Devil's dice – as Neville described them. She rolled every number she needed, all of the time. When they finally stopped playing in favour of having dinner the German beauty collected – most of it from a once-again irritated Neville – the healthy sum of two thousand, two hundred and sixty dollars.

When, dressed for dinner in evening clothes in true Orient Express style, they took their seats in the dining car, there was a brief passport inspection at the border town of Feldkirch.

Frannie's nerves jangled when the customs officer looked at her passport, although she had considered it a minimal risk to be re-entering Switzerland on the express – why should her name be at entry points? she had decided. Why, indeed, should it have been connected to the grisly events at the Villa du lac? – she nevertheless appreciated that there was that possibility.

As it was the officer treated her passport to the most cursory of inspections. When he moved on, Neville – who had pointed out that von Schwerin had a very powerful motive to keep quiet about the matter – gave her a reassuring smile. 'You see?' he said.

As she slipped her passport back into her evening bag, relieved, she had a fleeting impression that Giovanni gave her an oddly searching look, but then he said, 'May I choose the wine? The italian wines on this train are magnificent,' and she forgot about it.

The thickly juicy Salice Salentino, a rich red – like the food on that most sybaritic of trains – was indeed superb. After what had ultimately been a tiring session of backgammon, dinner revived them and the mood became firstly convivial and, after a while, wantonly playful. The sexual atmosphere between Frannie, Neville and Sandra thickened; they had, after all, enjoyed each other's bodies to the full in rare and stimulating ways and there was the imminent prospect of further dalliance. Giovanni – Frannie speculated – must have been growing curious as to their relationship since Neville, who was clearly squiring Sandra, paid just as much solicitous and affectionate attention to Frannie as her, whilst she appeared to be taking more than a passing interest in the Italian himself.

In the cosseted intimacy of the dining car, having been in close proximity to Giovanni all afternoon, Frannie was becoming more and more curious about the sexual possibilities of the man.

Wine loosened tongues; the steady motion of

the speeding express, the comforting thrumming of the wheels, the mystery of the passing darkness beyond the windows – all contributed to totally relax the four; it became clearer by the minute to the Italian that his companions were currently indulging in a three-way sexual relationship into which he was being seduced.

Once steered very firmly into the subject of sex, the conversation became rapidly bolder until Neville laid his cards on the table by remarking, most casually, 'Frannie and I and Sandra made love together last week.' He eyed Giovanni keenly then asked him, 'Do you go for that sort of thing?'

'Should I get the chance. It is not a thing which happens so very often.' He produced his boyish smile of innocence.

Frannie's hand fell suggestively on his satiny sleeve. 'I, um, I think you might *just* get that chance quite soon,' she said softly, thus firmly dispelling any doubts he might have had about the course the evening was about to take.

'But I am an Italian,' he told her, clean-cut face serious but deep brown eyes twinkling as they wandered over her face, '. . . a romantic. A new woman, it pleases me to wine her, to dine her, to romance her with music and moonlight and candles.' His eyes locked on hers, bringing a little thrill to her belly. 'The first time that I make love to her it is slowly, tenderly, with rising passion. This, you must understand, is an art which comes with my Latin blood. However, what you are now suggesting – am I right? – is that we four have sex together. That is something very different, is it not?'

'It is, baby, it is. No?' crooned Sandra. She

chuckled dirtily.

Stroking his sleeve, eyes remaining fixed on his, Frannie said, 'We *have* wined and dined, there's soft music, a candle on the table and somewhere out there is the moon. You don't like the idea of what comes next?'

His hand took a warm hold of the back of hers. 'We also have fire in our blood. Of course I like the idea. You talk raw sex to me, no romance. Is something else.' He paused, eyes running briefly over her breasts before returning to hers. 'It is a perversion.'

'Only of the most harmless kind.'

'You people perhaps go in for sadism, too?' There was a new light in his eyes.

Frannie's heart skipped a beat. 'Just the fun variety.'

'And you, Neville?'

Neville's gaze fell on Frannie as he remembered his session with her and Victor and the riding crops. He cracked a twisted grin. 'Yeah,' he drawled. 'Now and then I guess, yeah.'

There was no longer any need to entice Giovanni into their pending debauch; his entire demeanour had subtly changed. He was suddenly the one who seemed to be leading the way. Boldly, he said, 'Then should we all have some of the fun variety of sadism this evening?'

Frannie, pulse quickening, raised an eyebrow. 'What do you suggest?'

He glanced from her to Sandra and back again. His boyish look had vanished, his lips tightened; there was a tic in his cheek. 'Forgive me, but it seems to me that you are two very wanton ladies.'

He turned his eyes on Neville, narrowing them slightly. 'Such women are deserving of a certain amount of punishment, would you not agree, my friend?'

The American was in the act of lighting an after-dinner cigar. His gold Dupont, aflame, hovered near the Havana's end as his gaze wandered over first Sandra, then Frannie. 'I would. I certainly would,' he drawled. 'So how about we all have ourselves another sniff of booze, then we'll retire to my cabin and thrash their wicked butts?'

Sandra squealed loudly enough to attract the attention of nearby diners. 'You would not dare such a thing,' she said, eyes lustfully laughing.

'Too right I wouldn't.'

'Have a care, Neville darling, I bite,' said Frannie, getting randily in the mood.

'Not as hard as my belt, honey.' She wriggled her bottom saucily.

They were all slightly tipsy as they made their way in Indian file from the dining car and along the two carriages which separated it from the sleepers. The train was not moving; it was eleven twenty-five and the express was spending its scheduled twenty minutes at Flughafen Station in Zurich. Frannie, too filled with wine and the tingling anticipation of the upcoming frolic to be bothered by the fact that they were stopped but a fast twenty minutes drive from Villa du Lac, could almost feel Giovanni's eyes stripping away her Karl Lagerfeld dress and Coco Chanel knickers as he followed her through the train.

Neville's sleeping compartment had little to

distinguish it from Frannie's except that his complimentary bowl of fruit contained apples and bananas whereas her's had grapes. The bunk beds were neatly made, the coverlets turned back, and there was a gold-foil-wrapped chocolate on each pillow. As he locked the door on them, Neville commented, 'Hardly room to swing a cat in here.'

'But just enough to swing a belt, I think,' said Giovanni.

The Italian's intentions were not immediately of the flagellation variety; taking Frannie into his arms he pressed his lips on hers. She pushed her body close into him. Since he was a little shorter than her, she kicked off her high-heeled shoes; groin matched groin, the black sateen of her skirt was as thin as the silk of his evening trousers. Her curious sensitive crotch detected an arousingly large sexual package, the penis still softish but on the rise.

As Frannie and Giovanni passionately kissed there was a swishing noise; Neville had closed the curtain. 'We happen to be in a station, Frannie,' he said.

She broke the kiss. 'So?'

'You want to put on a show?'

She grinned, and shrugged carelessly as she ground her crotch into Giovanni's; Frannie was in scampish, raunchy mood. 'Why not?'

'Okay, be a porn star, honey,' he said, faintly slurring his words. 'That is, if you've got the balls.'

'Don't be vulgar.'

He reopened the curtain. There was a scattering

187

of people on the spotless flower-bedecked platform. As a strolling, sombrely dressed couple
approached the window of the cabin, Neville said,
'So why don't you take your dress off?'

'Want to see my balls, do you?'

She did not hesitated. Stooping and crossing her
hands in front of her she took hold of the hem of
Herr Lagerfeld's expensive creation and hauled
the dress over her head and off, mussing her loose
hair in the process. Having looked forward to a
night of sex, she had chosen appropriate lingerie;
she was wearing high-cut, see-through lace
knickers embroidered with large, blue flowers, a
matching corset-style bodice slung under her
naked breasts, sheer pale-blue stockings with frilly
white garter tops, and thin blue suspenders with a
belt in the same fashion as the garters.

The Swiss gentleman's eyes popped as the
couple walked by the window; his wife glared and
dragged him away. Neville's muttered, 'Have a
good evening' was fortunately too quiet for them
to hear.

'The lady is truly bad,' commented Giovanni. He
unbuckled his crocodile belt.

'She is, she is,' agreed Frannie, pulse pounding
as she watched him slip the belt from its loops. 'Ah
– bot thrashing time, is it?'

'You know it.'

'Then, maybe you'd better *close* the curtain again
Neville? That is, now that you've seen my balls?'

The American's laugh was short and hornily
thick. He did not bother to shut the curtain since
the train gave a lurch and was on the move. The
impossibly immaculate Flughafen Station slid by

as Neville now began to take off his belt – a heavyish black leather one. 'Let's whup both of them together?' he suggested to the Italian.

Sandra, who had been perching on the lower bunk, displayed unseemly enthusiasm; she happily dragged one of the two pillows from the bed. The chocolate hit the floor with a faint thump. 'On our knees, perhaps? You like?' she purred.

'Yeah. On your pretty knees, kid,' grunted Neville. He took hold of the other pillow and dropped it on the floor by the side of the bed, then moved the trolley with the flowers and fruit out of the way, across to the washstand.

'Next to one another, then? Bent over the bed, yes?' said Giovanni as he doubled his belt.

The express was gathering speed; the station was behind them, the lights of night-time Zurich hurrying by. Keyed up to a high pitch of excitement, Frannie knelt on a pillow as Sandra got down beside her. She wrapped an arm around the girl's bare shoulders, snuggling in tight to her, kissing her on the lips. 'You're obviously going to enjoy this as much as I am,' she whispered.

'You bet,' muttered Sandra. She tongued Frannie's lips.

Frannie wiggled her bottom as her flimsy knickers were seized and yanked down her thighs. Whilst lustily mingling tongues with Sandra she clearly heard above the steady thrumming of the train wheels the swish of tussah sliding against nylon as Neville dragged Sandra's tight, beige skirt over her hips to reveal her delectable, pantiless, backside.

The German girl had again changed her

transfers; on one cheek of her bottom, the size of the base of a wine glass, appeared the snarling head of a tiger; on the other a pair of crimson pouting female lips.

The men, resplendent still in full black tie, silken trouser fronts tellingly bulging, ogled the delectably fuckable naked posteriors as they took their places on either side of the wetly kissing females. Neville nodded encouragement at Giovanni; the Italian raised his belt arm across his body until his hand was at his left shoulder, then brought the stiff strip of crocodile skin sharply down in a backhanded blow across Frannie's buttocks.

Frannie shrieked into Sandra's mouth. Her hand reflexively clawed the girl's upper arm. Her stockinged feet drummed into the gently rocking carpeted floor of the train as the cheeks of her behind trembled and a thin red line appeared across them both; the lapping of her tongue against Sandra's became even more feverish.

Neville took his time; he touched the flat of his doubled belt on the angry face – destined to become angrier – of the tiger, slowly raised the chunky leather to head height, paused to savour the moment then lashed into Sandra's bottom precisely across the tiger's snarling mouth.

She yelped. Her buttocks cringed as a vivid red slash mark welled on them. She bit her lower lip hard. But since – like Frannie – she was somewhat of an aficionado of the whip, the blow served to further inflame her libido. As the stinging pain subsided into a hot glow her right hand crept beneath Frannie's thigh and her fingers hooked into the aristocratic pussy.

Giovanni's turn. Another backhanded swipe, the belt whistling through the air to connect with a satisfying crack, reptilian skin slapping into cringing human hide.

Another – grateful – shriek from Frannie; another stripe, almost parallel to the first. Frannie's left hand now began to go to work on Sandra's pussy in much the same fashion as the girl's right was on her own, thumb gentling her clitoris, fingers probing soft warm wetness.

The men's ribald activity begins to drive them very quickly towards lustful peaks. The Italian – who, after all, unlike the American has no previous experience of these horny ladies – becomes particularly highly aroused; to be suddenly offered – never having seen them before – two such perfectly formed and wantonly presented bare female behinds, one of them framing a blonde-fuzzed pussy, the other, tantalisingly transferred, presenting the most sensual of copper-fringed cunt lips – whilst both vaginas are penetrated by the other female's fingers – is in itself a thrill salacious enough; to be, together with another male, thrashing those bottoms is an experience most pornographic. The man – who only *calls* himself Giovanni – has never been more rampant in his life.

Administering this beating is proving to be a sensational bonus to the Italian's covert intention for getting into a sexual relationship with Lady Ballington.

The double beating heats up, the smarting, reddening, multi-striped backsides heat up.

The men come to the boil.

They are lashing away together, sweating with their exertion, cracking the belts down fast and with utmost vigour across glowing, trembling, discolouring buttocks – though in fact causing no damage more than welt marks and a little bruising – and occasionally catching the girls blows across the backs of their thighs. They have been switching around, alternating targets, Sandra has already climaxed once with a drawn-out wail and a shudder which went right through her body, whilst Frannie is rapidly building towards orgasm with Sandra's fingers jerking in her like furious little pistons.

Giovanni can contain himself no longer; he drops his belt, rips open his flies and, with a piggish grunt, falls to his knees behind Frannie to thrust a cock as fat as the plump bananas on the trolley behind him into Frannie's pussy with a heave so strenuous that his scrotum, bulging over the top of his lowered underpants front, is flung between Frannie's thighs to bang against the edge of the bunk.

Frannie squeals louder than at any of the lashes. It is sublimely delicious, this unheralded penetration – and Sandra's fingers meanwhile keep up their frenzied wanking whilst jammed between the base of Giovanni's cock and his drooping testicles. My lady's belly is consumed with fire. Her mouth stills, crushed against Sandra's. She punches her fist three times, hard on the bed. Her feet convulse off the floor. She comes, gasping and grunting, into Sandra's lips.

Withdrawing his cock to the glans, as Sandra's fingers slip out of his target, the Italian heaves again – and this time his balls are already erupting before his cock is fully in. Frannie is climaxing still; the sudden warm stickyish liquid rush within her serves to prolong her orgasm. Giovanni slumps lifelessly forward, his unbuttoned evening jacket flopping half over Frannie's back, half over Sandra's, as Frannie's eyes close and she moans, intensely satisfied, into the pale orange mohair bed cover.

The Orient Express, as if having just been wracked with an orgasm of its own, has slowed to a crawl; it is trundling into Baden on its way to Basel and the Swiss border with France.

As the train creeps through the outskirts of Baden, Neville – perfectly visible to any keen-eyed observer from the houses near the railway lines – is clumsily climbing out of his trousers and underpants, having already slung his jacket on the upper bunk. In his haste, he almost rips off his shirt and bow tie. Naked but for his shoes and socks, hard-on quivering, he falls to his knees behind Sandra. He runs a salivary tongue over her hot, tasty buttocks, lapping at them as if trying to quench the fire in them and his raunchy thirst for intimate female flesh at the same time. He pulls Frannie's inert fingers from Sandra's pussy; her hand flops, palm outwards, down the side of the bed. Neville's rakish tongue then trails wetly down his girlfriend's bottom crack to pause briefly at the tiny pink hole, where it intrudes before worming on down and diving into her cunt.

It was just as well that the train accelerated before entering Baden Station; it was nearly midnight and the handful of good Swiss citizens awaiting the last regular connection down the line might have found the salacious sight of what was transpiring in the only one of the Orient Express's sleeping cars with its curtain open too much for their basically prim and proper natures.

Neville Duke's need to come became irrepressible. While next to him Giovanni, with a glazed expression, began to straighten off Frannie's back and sink to his haunches – his cock, barely wilted, pointing forwards through his gaping fly – he positioned himself behind Sandra, teased her bottom hole with the tip of his cock, squeezing it fractionally in there, before taking it out and ramming it into her pussy. He went at her with the speed and force of the connecting rods on the churning wheels below them, panting, sweating and grunting. As his come began to flood out of him he performed one of his favourite acts, withdrawing to direct the stream of sperm over her buttocks and the backs of her thighs; the final spurt soiled the tops of her stockings while she jerked her pelvis into the edge of the mattress as if fucking herself and came with a muffled shout into the side of her balled fist.

The four satiated bodies shook lazily with the motion of the express as it carved its way into the darkness beyond Baden. Giovanni's eyes slowly unglazed to focus on Frannie's gaping damp pussy and her thoroughly punished behind. They shifted to the same area of Sandra's anatomy then drifted to Neville who was sitting on the floor in his near nakedness, an arm draped over the piled skirt on Sandra's hips, a hand gripping his shrunken cock, his head back, his eyes closed.

Giovanni smiled in satisfaction; the night was progressing extraordinarily well. He would indulge himself sexually some more – this time with the delicious Sandra – before getting around to the very special business he had with Lady Ballington.

The Italian climbed to his feet and began to strip off; his stout cock, which had never fully lost its hard-on, was starting to go rigid again.

Frannie stirred. She reached behind her and smoothed a tortured buttock with the palm of her hand. Taking hold of her half-mast knickers, she began to haul them up: Giovanni's hand stopped her, insisting her own downwards.

'It is still early,' he said. 'Surely you are taking your panties in the wrong direction?'

She threw a bleary-eyed glance over her shoulder; for the first time she caught sight of the handsome cock which had brought her so rapidly to such a consuming orgasm. 'My, my,' she admiringly muttered, '. . . does that thing never go down?'

'Not until he is *fully* satisfied.' He closed in on her, holding his prick and running its distended head up and down her buttock cleft. 'And that takes a great deal more of fucking.'

'*Does* it? I do believe I'm glad about that.' She pulled her knickers down, raising each knee in turn to get them to her calves, then lifting her feet high to slip the knickers over them. He took them from her and thrust them to his nose, sniffing before dropping them on the floor.

'Dirty bastard.'

'You should know, *carina*.'

'No doubt I'm going to find out.'

Frannie straightened from the bed and began to stand. Though luxuriating in the aftermath of orgasm, she was already beginning to feel a delicious horniness creeping over her again.

'This without question. You are going to find out.' Giovanni's grin returned, rather less innocent than earlier, but boyish enough to successfully mask the true significance of his words.

Frannie perched on the bed next to recovering Sandra. 'Ouch. *Ow*! *Christ*!' went Sandra as she rubbed her buttocks, fingers slipping on an undried patch of Neville's sperm.

'You were more than keen to be thrashed,' said Giovanni. 'Now you are making a fuss about it.'

'It is bloody sore. It *hurts*. Christ!'

'It's supposed to. Quit complaining,' said the recuperated Neville.

Heat also seared Frannie's bottom as she shifted position on the bed. '*Yikes!*' she yelped, taking her weight on her hands.

'You too?' Neville laughed.

'But did I say I didn't like it?'

'Bet your sweet life you didn't.'

Neville got to his feet and went to the wash area to rummage in his toilet bag. He produced from it a plastic container of Nivea after-sun gel. 'In case you think I'm a totally heartless bastard, this is to soothe your butts.'

He had Sandra strip off her sadly crumpled dress and climb – still wearing her self-supporting stockings and high-heeled shoes – on to the upper bunk to lie flat on her belly while Frannie got supine on the lower bunk. He squeezed a copious amount of the thin pale-blue non-greasy jelly on to the cheeks of both their rear ends. 'Why don't you do Sandra, and I'll take care of Frannie?' he suggested to the Italian. He nodded at the man's swaying erection. 'Then I guess you'll want one of the chicks to take care of that.'

As he began to smooth the gel over and around Sandra's tiger's head, mixing it in with Neville's sperm, Giovanni asked Neville if the American would mind if he fucked his girlfriend.

'One of the reasons I invited you back with us, pal. But why don't you ask her? It's her fanny.'

'Would you like me to fuck you, Sandra?' said the Italian softly as he finished with one buttock and began spreading the gel over the one with the pouting red lips.

'Mmmm.' Sandra wriggled pleasurably as her flaming behind began to cool. He bent his head to move his lips close to her ear. His hand slipped deep within the cheeks of her bottom and a finger found its little hole, probing. 'May I put my dick in here?' he whispered.

'If you like,' she muttered, licking her lips.

As he attended to Frannie's burning buttocks, Neville's cock was gradually rising. Frannie was unaware of this because he was crouching by the bunk, his genitals out of sight; her centre of interest was the impressive equipment which had so recently given her such satisfaction. Giovanni's body was only visible to her from mid-thigh to shoulder since he was administering to Sandra above her – but that was really all she needed to see; his solid prick was bouncing intriguingly with the regular rocking motion of the train, and his balls shook.

The Italian's open palm made an appearance as he asked Neville for more of the gel. Neville filled it, then, to Frannie's slight regret, the genital display came to an end as Giovanni heaved himself up on to the bunk; the bed creaked, the brown velvet covering of the mattress above Frannie's head sagging with his added weight as he settled down with Sandra on a bunk meant only for one.

'Better?' asked Neville. He traced the tips of his fingers up over the knobs of Frannie's spine and under her flowing hair to caress the back of her neck.

She sighed. 'Sort of glowing, yet cool at the same time.'

'Lick my balls? Get it all the way up again and we'll have a nice slow easy fuck.'

The suddenness of the huskily delivered invitation sent a sexual thrill through Frannie's loins. She turned on to her side and raised her head, leaning over the edge of the bunk as Neville stood and closed in on her face, his knees slightly bent, a shock of hair curtaining his forehead. Taking hold of the three-quarter erect cock she lifted it until her knuckles were buried amongst Neville's forest of belly hairs. She salivated her tongue and scooped it under his heavy scrotum, licking noisily, aware of his prick thickening in her palm. Sucking one testicle completely inside her mouth she began to toss the American prick, revelling in its increasing rigidity, her nose bumping its base.

On the upper bunk, activity of a slightly more esoteric nature was under way; Giovanni had liberally smeared two of his fingers with gel and was rotating them, buried to the second knuckles, in Sandra's bottom hole. He gave them a final twist then removed the fingers and applied the remains of the gel to his rampant cock. Easing a buttercup pillow beneath Sandra's hips, he spread her legs until one of her feet was hanging over the edge of the bed and the other touching the compartment wall and rolled between them. Tensing, Sandra took hold of the edges of the pillow on which her cheek rested, nails biting into it. The Italian supported himself on one arm to fit his big cockhead into the crack of her behind, found her tiny hole with it and, most greedily intent on his buggery, began to stretch Sandra's sphincter.

Neville, meanwhile, was enjoying the double pleasure of being fellated by Frannie as at the same time he watched Giovanni with Sandra, on a level with his eyes; they ignored him.

Sandra moaned into the pillow. She scrunched two fistfuls of linen-filled down, her knuckles whitening, her sphincter protesting as Giovanni's cock relentlessly opened her bottom, forcing its lustful way in. Her legs jerked; one shoe fell off to clunk on the floor.

Giovanni paused in his effort, his glans deep enough in her to enable him to unhand his cock without it slipping out. Taking his weight on both arms he lowered his chest to Sandra's back and his mouth into the coppery curls masking her ear. 'You would like for me to stop?' he whispered. 'Is perhaps too much for you?'

'Is too much for me, *ja*. But do not fucking stop.' Sandra gasped into the pillow. 'I like!'

Too much for Sandra, it was clearly not; once her

sphincter was properly breached, moments later, pain subsided. Sweet, intense, forbidden pleasure took its place as the Latin dick shoved its dissolute way deep inside the tiny teutonic arsehole. Giovanni raised himself on straightened arms to feast his eyes on the progress of his sodomy. Only when his cock had entirely disappeared, his balls were nestled under Sandra's bottom, and his pubic bush flattened over her buttocks to touch both vivid transfers did Giovanni go still, wallowing in the very special thrill of having his stiff cock grasped from one end to the other as tightly as if it were a cork in a wine bottle.

Sandra shuddered; her bottom hole felt as filled as the neck of that bottle. One of her hands uncrunched the pillow and crawled down to her crotch where its fingers began to busy themselves with her needful clitoris as Giovanni withdrew his prick almost all the way out of its anal sheath, paused fractionally, then plunged again, preparing to get into the wanton rhythm of a hearty bum-fuck.

Frannie, with her mouth crammed with cock below them, has a view only of Sandra's stockinged foot and part of her shin – from which she understands that the girl is on her belly and – by the way her foot jerks and twitches – that she is being penetrated. She is visited by an irresistible yen to take a peek at the activity on the upper bunk. Unmouthing Neville, she stands, gets a hold of the wooden edge above her and pulls herself on to tiptoes.

The buggery is a truly lubricious sight which quickly stokes up the sexual fire in Frannie's loins;

with her wide-spread, stockinged legs and one shoe, her transferred, rosy, striped and bruised behind, Sandra presents an extraordinarily erotic picture as she ecstatically rolls her face around on the pillow, kicks her feet and grunts and moans while Giovanni's heavy prick steadily pumps in and out of her quivering bottom.

Neville gets behind Frannie. He grabs the insides of her thighs and parts them; for a moment, as she feels his cock pressing beneath her backside, she thinks he intends doing to her what they are witnessing in front of them. But he leaves her anus alone. He lets go of her thighs. One hand takes hold of his cock as the other slips around to her belly, then drops to her bush. Bending at the knees, he pokes his penis between her legs, hooks the fingers of his pussy-caressing hand beneath his glans, eases it into Frannie's cunt and thrusts his cock all the way up her. She briefly screws her eyes shut as a wave of pleasure surges through her loins then, as Neville begins to energetically fuck her, she opens them on the top-bunk buggery.

The double stimulation of voyeurism – and Giovanni and Sandra are so engrossed in their ribald activity that they give no indication of being aware they are being watched – and a 'knee-trembler' are wildly exciting for both Frannie and Neville; Frannie's orgasm steadily builds. Glancing down, she sees the American's balls fast-jiggling between her parted thighs. But she ogles this ruttish sight only for seconds because the sexual noises emanating from the couple in front of her – rising to almost drown out the dull clatter of the speeding train – spell imminent climax;

Frannie's eyes latch greedily on to Giovanni's bouncing buttocks.

So busy has Sandra's hand become beneath her that her arm shudders as if she is operating a pneumatic drill. She has her face turned towards Frannie, her cheek crushed into the pillow, her eyes closed, and she is grunting staccato sounds – 'ah, oo, oo, oo, ah, ah . . .' as Giovanni ramrods her rear end, panting like a dog with each thrust.

Sandra's grunts merge into a drawn-out, orgiastic moan and her arm stills as Giovanni throws back his head and howls – a wolf to the moon – his strong buttocks going rigid, thigh muscles bulging, sperm pumping into Sandra's backside with his final sodomitic heaves. He collapses, his weight pressing Sandra into the mattress; overwhelmed with the salacity of observing this while a cock slams into her pussy from behind, Frannie comes with a noisy whimper.

Neville has not yet made it – and his legs are fast tiring. Slipping his length out of Frannie he lies down on the bunk and pulls her on top of him. Muttering, 'Your turn to do some work, honey,' he fists his cock back inside her pussy.

Frannie, appetite still ravenous, rides Neville like a wildcat; she revels in this variation where she takes charge of the fucking and can go at it at the speed of her choosing. Her eyes lech on her penetrated jerking cunt through jiggling tits and flying necklace.

Neville had brought himself almost to the brink of orgasm whilst doing it standing up and almost immediately he erupts inside disappointed Frannie. She attempts to speedily bring herself off again with her bouncing, but her flesh-pole loses its rigidly and soon she has nothing to bounce on.

There is an irritating gentle snore from the American's lips; Frannie rolls off him on to her back, uncomfortably aware of the fragility and tenderness of her buttocks against the counterpane, and begins to needfully play with herself.

'You perhaps would like a little help with that?' murmured Giovanni, peering down from the upper bunk. Momentarily – oddly, considering the situation – embarrassed to be caught masturbating, Frannie slid her hand from her pussy and down the inside of her thigh, saying nothing, smiling thinly.

'He is asleep, I see, your friend.'

'Yes.'

'The trouble with Americans. No staying power.'

'I wouldn't exactly say that.'

'Sandra, she is asleep too.'

'Is she?' Frannie was looking up into a face which – last seen by her contorted with lust – had miraculously regained all its boyishness.

Giovanni grinned. 'That leaves you and me.' His eyes meaningfully latched on to Frannie's pussy; her hand had crept back up her thigh to rest inactively on it. 'Clearly, you are in need of more sex.'

Her pussy contracted briefly. 'Maybe.'

'You are – as am I.'

Hairy legs intruded over the edge of the bed. The naked Italian launched himself to the floor, his big cock flopping upwards to slap at his belly as he did so. 'But,' he said, '. . . they are both asleep and there is so little room.' He found his underpants and began to climb into them. 'Let us dress and go to *my* cabin. Come.'

It was almost a command – at the very least it sounded as if the man had no doubt whatsoever that Frannie would agree.

And of course she did.

Perversely, she remembered – most fortunately for her as it was to turn out – the equipment she had neglected to bring to Neville's cabin, her video bag. She fumbled on the floor for her knickers.

'Okay,' Frannie breathed, pussy egging her on, '. . . but we'll go to my cabin, if it's all the same to you.'

She did not bother with putting her knickers on; she stuffed them into her evening bag. As Giovanni hurried into his clothes, she dragged the Lagerfeld dress over her head to pull it down to cover her cute bodice; she smoothed the skirt over the suspender belt and pale blue stockings.

Lady Ballington was most anxious to get rid of the dress again and get it together once more with the macho Italian.

12

MURDER ON THE ORIENT EXPRESS!

IT WAS NOT FAR TO GO – just six doors along the swaying rumbling corridor. They encountered no one, which was perhaps just as well since Frannie was barefoot, carrying her shoes, and Giovanni had not bothered to button or tuck in his shirt. Frannie's bottom fiercely smarted as her bare haunches rubbed against sateen; but her pussy was its usual, eager self and the heat in her buttocks served to remind her of the excitement of the beating and thus inflame her libido even further.

It was one forty-five, the express would shortly be through Basel and into La Belle France.

With them locked in her sleeping car, the first thing Frannie did was to take a tissue from her video bag so that she could covertly angle the fruit and drinks trolley so that the lens was on the bed, and set the film rolling. Then she fell into the Italian's arms.

As they voraciously kissed, Giovanni rucked up her dress behind until the sateen was bunched in his hand above her bare bottom. He took hold of a sore buttock with the other hand, his fingertips deep in her cleft, and gently squeezed.

'How does it feel, this gorgeous behind of

yours?' he asked her.

She pressed her crotch hard into his. 'You're the one who's feeling it,' she throatily, jokily replied.

'You enjoy many such things kinky?' His middle finger probed her bottom hole as his pinky teased her cunt.

'Such as?'

'Bondage, perhaps?'

'When the mood grabs me.'

He fell to his knees at her feet. Letting the skirt go so that it dropped into place behind her, he hauled it up in front to her belly with both hands to expose, inches from his twitching nose, her pussy. After gazing at it for several seconds he dipped his tongue there, flattening the little heap of skirt against her suspender belt so that he was able to stare into her eyes as he licked her.

Her knees sagged; she made little mewling noises. The tongue probed deeply into her dampness then slipped out, its tip teasing her clitoris.

'So how *is* the mood?' he asked. He trailed his tongue through her pubic thatch until it met the fine line of hairs which led to her navel.

'It's – grabbing,' she muttered, raring for some more sexual fun and games before the main event.

'Good.' His tongue briefly lapped her pussy again, then he got to his feet. He took her dress with him to pull it up and over her head. 'With your permission, I shall tie you up.'

'Oh,' went Frannie, feebly.

Throwing the dress so that it piled up by the

outside carriage door, he reached behind her and unhooked the little bodice. 'For this, you should be naked.'

'Whatever turns you on. I understood men liked women dressed in bits and pieces of frippery?'

'Men also like women to be nude.'

'Okay.' She unclipped a stocking and began to roll it down, watching him watching her as she did so. 'Women also like men to be nude.'

'If you wish.'

By the time she had both stockings off he was naked, his evening suit on one of her hangers, his white slips on the floor. 'Lie on the bed,' he told her.

Mightily aroused, pulse beginning to race, noting that his fat and sturdy cock was fully erect, she sat on the edge of the bunk then rolled on to her back. He picked up her stockings from where they lay close to his underpants. 'I'll use these, okay?'

'Okay,' she muttered.

Hovering over her, his genitals wobbling tantalisingly as the train, slowing down through Basel, began to rock more, he tied her wrists, hands palm to palm, in front of her. He glanced out at the passing lights and moved to close the curtain. Then he tied her feet and her knees with the other stocking and for good measure secured the end of the one trailing from her wrists around the stretched silk at her knees.

With Lady Ballington tightly trussed with her own pale-blue stockings, the Orient Express rumbled to a shuddering halt. As Giovanni stood back to lustily admire his handiwork, a nearby door creaked open; Basel was a customs point, but there would be no attempt to disturb them since they had earlier handed in their declarations and passports to their cabin steward.

'I did lock us in?' asked Frannie.

He checked. 'You did.'

'Now what? How are you going to make love to me with my legs closed?'

'I'll manage. But let us wait until we are out of Switzerland and in Marquis de Sade country.'

A touch of alarm clouded her face. 'But I don't want to be beaten any more. I've had enough.' She raised her hips to shift position in an attempt to make her backside more comfortable.

'I am only going to make you wait. Is that not what bondage is supposed to be all about?'

Climbing on to the bed, Giovanni straddled her body, facing her. He took hold of his cock and jerked his fist on it, balls hanging between her breasts. As there was the muted thumping of passing shoes in the corridor he said, 'But while you wait I propose to make a little love to your breasts. Then you can suck me.'

She forgot her throbbing bottom as she watched him flatten his erection up between her tits. With both hands he crushed her breasts together until their nipples touched and all that could be seen by her of his fleshily buried cock was its huge glans, pointing at her lips, with its little hole slightly open.

He began to rock his hips, lower buttocks sliding on her belly as his prick rode up and down in its carnal enclosure. Frannie craned her neck to stretch out her tongue so that every time the Italian cock was thrust fully forward, five inches or more of it visible, his balls tucked up into her breasts, she could wet the glans with saliva and tease its opening.

A door banged closed. The compartment lurched, a whistle blew, and the train began to move, quickly gathering speed out of Basel Station.

Giovanni moved, too. He shifted himself forward with his weight on his knees on either side of Frannie's shoulders so that his genitals hung over her face, massive at such close quarters. Thrusting his cock in her mouth he began to do to it what he had been doing to her tits, steadily fucking it, rocking inches of it in and out. Desperately craving to masturbate while she gave head, Frannie could only manage to rub the sides of her tied hands on her pubic bush.

'We must be in France now,' Giovanni muttered, minutes later.

Frannie tried to say 'Fuck me,' into her mouthful of penis.

He must have understood, because he said, 'I think it is time.'

Backing his cock out of her mouth, he rolled it against one cheek, then the other, had her lick his balls, then he climbed off her. He pushed her on to her side to face the compartment partition wall.

'Aren't you going to untie me?' Frannie gasped, as he began to tuck his body into her back, cockhead bumping her behind.

'I do it like this.'

For the second time that evening, she thought

209

he was going to bugger her. But instead he took hold of the soft flesh of the upper backs of her thighs, close to her plump little pussy lips, and used it as handles to spread her vulva. He eased his glans into her wetness and shoved, prick sliding full length inside her, balls crushing into the backs of her thighs.

'So tight like this,' he breathed. 'Almost as tight as Sandra's little backside. Beautiful.'

Frannie cannot remember ever having had coitus like this. Her buttocks are so tender that with each pelvic thrust, as Giovanni's wiry pubic hairs push into them it feels almost as if she is getting another taste of the belt. With her legs trussed together the Italian cock fills her wonderfully. Climax begins to build, discomfort forgotten.

Giovanni draws fast towards orgasm; this lovely lady is one of the most attractive he has ever had the good fortune to dally with – she has turned him on incredibly.

The Italian deeply regrets what it is he is obliged to do to Frannie shortly. Sadly, it is the way of the world.

His fucking gathers momentum. Her bottom, careless of tenderness, heaves to meet each powerful thrust, her tied hands, jammed between her legs, saw against her pussy, her tits bounce and jiggle, she pants and drools like an overheated animal.

Frannie comes a half a minute ahead of him. Relaxing in the euphoric afterglow of orgasm, she is treated to the good feeling of his seed – it is amazing how much of it there is – spilling into her pussy and hitting the entrance to her womb.

Huddled behind her, his cock slowly shrinking within her, Giovanni holds Frannie very fiercely, as an unhappy child might cling on to its mother. His front is sticky with perspiration against her back; his chest slightly wheezes as his breathing settles down.

Fighting against the nervousness which habitually attacks him at such moments, he breaks away, rolls off the bed and goes to the outside window. Opening the curtain, he slides the window halfway down – as far as it will go for reasons of safety. Cold night air rushes into the compartment; the thundering sound of the train is magnified.

Frannie shivers. She contrives herself on to her back. 'What are you doing that for?' she mumbles.

'It is hot. A little air.'

'It's enough, for God's sake!'

He picks his white slips off the floor and perches with them in his hand on the edge of the bed as the chilly air of the French countryside continues to whistle in, bringing with it a faint smell of cattle.

'You are a most lovely lady,' he tells her. 'But now I am afraid I am going to do something to you which I am going to detest. Frannie, believe me, I am most truly sorry.'

Alarm bells begin to ring in Frannie's ears then jangle frightfully as the Italian forces his underpants around her mouth, drags their sides behind her head and gags her with them.

'If I could back out of my contract, believe me, I would. But it is too late.' His schoolboy face looks infinitely troubled and sad. 'Hired killers with

Mafia connections do that only once before being killed themselves.' He pauses. 'This is for Wolfgang von Schwerin.'

Giovanni kisses Frannie's forehead most tenderly as, stunned, realising only at that moment the full, dreadful significance of the man's words and actions, Frannie reaches her thumb to the emerald ring and turns its stone.

'I am sorry,' repeats the Italian. He adds, the words horrifically chilling, 'At least you were enjoying a fuck to the very end.' He picks her up to swing her effortlessly off the bed as she kicks her feet and screams into his underpants.

Gregory happened to be awake and reading a Norman Mailer novel when his bleeper screeched. '*Christ!*' he bellowed.

He leapt from his bed. Barefoot and barechested, wearing just a pair of jeans, he wrenched open the door of his compartment; an entire carriage separated it from that of Frannie.

Gregory charged along his corridor, had a brief tussle with the communicating door, thundered on.

The hired assassin bundled trussed and naked Frannie feet first through the open window. The train was travelling at one hundred and fifty kilometres per hour through the rugged countryside of Haute-Saône: at such a speed she would have not the faintest chance of survival.

Lady Ballington's death was seconds away.

Gregory furiously rattled the sleeping compartment door before smashing the glass with his bare elbow and reaching through to unlock it, the racket of his actions sufficient for Giovanni, trampling Frannie's dress underfoot, about to launch her into eternity, to pause with her half in, half out of the window and throw a startled glance over his shoulder.

Seething with anger, powerful – at that moment – as a charging bull, Gregory was on him and dragging Frannie back through the window and out of his grasp. He flung his mistress on the bed. Unstoppable in his rage, he turned on the far shorter Italian, smashed him around the face with a karate chop and swore, 'You fucking murderous *bast*ard!'

As another wave of rage even more violent than the first tore through him, he stooped, took the dazed assassin by the back of his knees, lifted him and tipped him backwards into space.

He went in silence, vanishing into the night.

Gregory did not even bother to glance out of the window; he slammed it closed. Panting, fighting for breath, he turned baleful eyes on Frannie. After long moments he muttered, 'Man overboard. Pity.' His gaze swept over her. 'Jesus, Lady B.,' he grunted. '*Jesus*!'

The corridor door was open, there was glass on the carpet. Gregory stuck his head out; by some miracle the noise seemed to have disturbed no one. His temper beginning to calm, he quietly closed the door. Going to Frannie, he untied her would-be killer's underpants from her mouth; holding them at arms length he stared at them in distaste. His eyes fell on the hanger with Giovanni's suit on it, the shirt hanging over one shoulder, the bow tie draping out of a pocket.

As Frannie, silent, struggling to calm her

bowstring nerves, watched him, he took the clothes to the window, reopened it and threw them item by item into the darkness. He sent the man's shoes and socks after them, shut the window and the curtain and replaced the hanger.

Frannie found her voice. 'What, what did you do that for?' she stammered.

'Silly question.' He set to work, eyes averted from her nakedness, freeing her.

Rubbing her shoulder where it had banged into the wall as a result of the violence with which Gregory had flung her on to the bed, she grumbled, 'I'm not a bloody sack of potatoes.'

''alf a second more and you would 'ave been as good as, ma'am.' He untied the final knot.

'I know it, I didn't mean to complain. It's just that . . .' she covered her nakedness with a sheet. 'God, that was horribly close.'

He ran a weary, cynical eye over her. 'Then again, it always is, isn't it?'

She sighed. 'But why *me*?'

'*Hah*! Another silly question. Won't you *never* learn, Lady Ballington?'

'That will *do*, thank you, Gregory,' she told him, severely.

She mouthed a wry nervous little smile.

13

EXPRESS DIARY

I USED TO *LIKE* TRAINS!

Can you imagine? That was supposed to be a quiet, relaxing, luxurious trip on the world's most famous train – with a soupçon of sex thrown in here and there, naturally. I should really stay home and take up knitting.

We got off in Paris where I had the Learjet pick us up and fly us home. I had been at Stratton Castle only a day or so when a couple of gentlemen from Interpol, as part of their routine questioning of all passengers on Orient Express the night that the mangled naked body of a suspected Mafia hit-man was discovered by the tracks close to Lure visited me. Of course, it immediately became perfectly clear to them that the noble wife of one of England's richest men could not possibly have been mixed up in so sordid an event and they quickly left.

I suppose that had Agatha Christie penned the story, the good Inspector Poirot would have solved the mystery: '*Cherchez la femme*,' he would have concluded; 'ze sleeping car of ze victim was locked on ze outside, ergo 'e was disposed of through ze window of another compartment; his body 'ad upon it traces of perfume, there was a smear of lipstick on 'is underpants, therefore 'e 'ad been with a woman; his clothes were thrown from ze train after 'im – murder without doubt; crime passionel, per'aps, my friends?; ze sleeping compartment of ze most attractive Lady Ballington was broken into on ze same night yet she registered no complaint; a jealous lover, n'est-ce pas?'

Slightly cack-handed reasoning but nevertheless I would have been hauled before the French courts and the truth would have come out.

Fortunately, Inspector Poirot does not work for Interpol.

I get an attack of the horrors every time I consider what might have been the outcome had I not taken the Italian back to my cabin because I wanted to video what happened between us; we would have gone, as he had suggested, to *his* cabin and I doubt if Gregory would have found it in time to save my life.

Talking of videos, as far as that unhinged murderer von Schwerin is concerned, I did send a copy of the soundtrack of my final session with him to the Swiss police, giving them the exact information of what transpired, but being most careful that they should not get the slightest clue as to my identity. He is in prison now, awaiting trial on the strength of it; I suspect and hope he will end his days in a lunatic asylum.

So. Another adventurous sex tale reaches its end. I am *drained*! Not surprising when you know that I go through all the emotions over again when writing about my experiences.

Did you get off on my story here and there? I

pray that you did, or else what was the point of me writing it?

Maybe I'll stay home from now on. Maybe. But somehow I doubt it.

Ciao.

F.

☐	Frannie	Francesca Jones	£4.99
☐	Frannie Rides Again	Francesca Jones	£4.99
☐	Frannie Rides Out	Francesca Jones	£4.50
☐	Frannie Goes to Hollywood	Francesca Jones	£4.50
☐	Erotic Fantasies	Iris & Steven Finz	£4.99
☐	The Best Sex I Ever Had	Iris & Steven Finz	£4.50
☐	Delicious Sex	Gael Greene	£4.99
☐	Nine and a Half Weeks	Elizabeth McNeill	£4.99

Warner now offers an exciting range of quality titles by both established and new authors which can be ordered from the following address:

Little, Brown and Company (UK)
P.O. Box 11,
Falmouth,
Cornwall TR10 9EN.

Alternatively you may fax your order to the above address. Fax No. 0326 376423.

Payments can be made as follows: cheque, postal order (payable to Little, Brown and Company) or by credit cards, Visa/Access. Do not send cash or currency. UK customers and B.F.P.O. please allow £1.00 for postage and packing for the first book, plus 50p for the second book, plus 30p for each additional book up to a maximum charge of £3.00 (7 books plus).

Overseas customers including Ireland, please allow £2.00 for the first book plus £1.00 for the second book, plus 50p for each additional book.

NAME (Block Letters) ....

....

ADDRESS ....

....

....

☐ I enclose my remittance for _____

☐ I wish to pay by Access/Visa Card

Number ☐☐☐☐☐☐☐☐☐☐☐☐☐☐☐☐☐☐

Card Expiry Date ☐☐☐☐